HIGH SUM~~MER~~ at ~~Aughris Farm but~~ Fionuala
is depressed.

Vera Pettigrew

FIONUALA 🌸 THE 🌸 GLENDALOUGH GOAT GOES WEST

Illustrated by Terry Myler

THE CHILDREN'S PRESS

To Stanley

First published 1994 by
The Children's Press
45 Palmerston Road, Dublin 6.

© Text: Vera Pettigrew
© Illustrations: The Children's Press

ISBN 0 974962 85 9

Typeset by Computertype Limited
Printed by Colour Books, Dublin

Contents

1 Friends 7
2 The Plan 13
3 The Journey Begins 21
4 The Zoo 27
5 Nightmares 33
6 Nooly 40
7 Puck Fair 46
8 By Boat to Lahinch 53
9 Galway 63
10 The Connemara Pony Show 69
11 Westport House 75
12 Sligo 83
13 Woodville Farm 90
14 Knocknarea 97
15 Coney Island 102
16 Lough Gill 109
17 Parke's Castle 116
18 Home 126
Map 48–49

1

Friends

Fionuala dozed in the drowsy heat. Up above in a blue sky larks sang, while swifts swooped and dived screaming, their long wings slicing through the warm air. The perfume of wild flowers drifted down the valley, while Sugarloaf Mountain shimmered in haze. Summer had come.

On Sugarloaf Farm the goats grazed the green pasture, their babies skipping beside them. That year Fionuala had no baby – not that she minded, for kids could be a nuisance at times. A fly buzzed by, tickling her ears, while a frog, slippery yellow, jumped at her feet, but she was so deep in thought she didn't notice, for Fionuala was depressed.

'What's wrong with her?' wondered the goats when they saw her downcast face and sad eyes. 'Is she ill?'

'She's missing Daniel, her son,' whispered Siobhan, Fionuala's friend.

As Fionuala stood in the warm sunshine, tears ran down her face and fell on the soft grass as she thought of her beautiful white kid who had grown up handsome and strong. But he had become so naughty that the farmer said he must go. Fionuala was sad when his new owners came for him but then he wrote letters of his home in Sligo and she was happy. Time passed and no more letters came and she grew depressed again.

From across the valley came a sound. It drifted over the fields and the woods, and as Fionuala heard it she lifted her head and her eyes brightened – Jacko was calling.

'I'm coming,' she answered and down the mountainside she ran, leaving the herd behind.

Once Fionuala had gone on a journey. She had travelled through County Wicklow, meeting people and animals and making friends, but her greatest friend of all was Jacko, the singing donkey. Together they walked the roads of Wicklow until Fionuala found what she was searching for – her relations, the Cool-Boys of Glendalough. When the great journey was over and Fionuala returned home to Sugarloaf Farm, Jacko went to live across the valley at Enniskerry House. He was happy there but sometimes he grew lonely. Then he would lift his large black head with the two long ears, and he would give a great 'hee-haw' which rolled across the valley, shattering the peace of the countryside. Fionuala would leave Sugarloaf Farm and travel the mile or two to Enniskerry House to see him.

At first the farmer was angry at her comings and goings but as time passed he grew used to her ways. Fionuala was a great cyclist and sometimes she borrowed the farmer's bike.

But it was old and rickety and very tiring to ride. Then one day she found in the shed a lovely new red bike, with a basket on the handlebars, and a shiny silver bell. Of course, it wasn't for her at all; it was for the farmer's wife but, as she seldom rode it, Fionuala considered it was hers. Every goat on Sugarloaf Farm came running to admire it, except

Big Bill, and he wouldn't even look at it. Fionuala didn't like Big Bill; he was a bossy guy. So she cycled up and down past his shed, ringing her bell loudly, until Big Bill flew into a towering rage. He kicked and stamped his stable door until it shivered and shook.

As Fionuala rode out of the yard on that warm summer day to visit Jacko, Big Bill was watching.

'Off to see the old ass?' he called.

'That's none of your business, silly Billy,' answered Fionuala as she pedalled out through the gate, narrowly missing a passing car.

Down the hill she went with the wind whistling past. She was going so fast that she nearly rode right into the farmer who was walking slowly up the hill.

'Look where you're going,' he shouted but Fionuala was already out of sight. Zooming round

corners, up and down the hills she rode, until in no time at all she reached the gates of Enniskerry House. Beside them was a gatelodge and a sign which said:

SEE THE GARDENS OF ENNISKERRY HOUSE
ADMISSION £2

But Fionuala had no money. In the past she had crept in when no one was looking, pushing her way through a hedge. Once she had even dug a hole under the gate and crawled in. She did so much damage and was such a nuisance that in the end they let her in, free, whenever she wanted.

She pushed open the gates, as a man looked out of the lodge window.

'Close them,' he called, but Fionuala had gone.

'Dratted goat,' he muttered as he banged them shut.

Down the avenue of tall trees Fionuala cycled. She smelt the garlic and the wild flowers. A little rabbit waved as she cycled by, while his parents in the long grass peered out.

'There goes the old goat,' they said. 'She looks sad today.'

A wood-pigeon in a tall tree called 'coo-ee', but Fionuala didn't answer.

As she turned the last corner she could see Jacko, head down, moving slowly over the green lawn, for after a lifetime of work all he did now was eat!

'What took you so long?' he called as she cycled up.

As they sat under a tall lime-tree, Jacko tried to cheer her up.

'You're getting yourself into a state about nothing,' he said. 'Daniel is well able to take care of himself.'

'But he hasn't written lately,' fretted Fionuala.

'You know how careless kids get about keeping in touch,' said Jacko. Privately he thought that Daniel had been spoilt silly and it didn't surprise him that he had stopped writing.

'Oh, Jacko!' Two big tears rolled down Fionuala's cheeks. 'I'm so worried. If only I knew that he was all right. He could be lying dead somewhere.'

'Or just gone to the bad, more likely,' thought Jacko, though he didn't say anything.

'If only I could see him, then I'd be satisfied,' said Fionuala.

'You'll have to find him first,' said Jacko.

'That's it!' Fionuala sat bolt upright. A thought had just come into her head and a very exciting thought it was. 'Jacko,' she said, 'I'll go in search of him, and you must come too.'

The bees hummed in the lime-tree and a pheasant called, as Jacko fell silent.

'I can't go,' he said at last. 'It's not possible.'

'Why not?' asked Fionuala. 'A holiday would do you good.'

'Who would eat the lawns?' replied Jacko. 'I have an important job to do here.'

'There are lawn-mowers in the shed,' said Fionuala, 'and you're getting fat,' and indeed he was. 'You need exercise.'

'Fionuala,' said Jacko, alarmed at the turn the conversation was taking, 'how could we find him? We don't even know where he is.'

'Oh, but I do. He's in Sligo. That's not a very big

place. Someone is sure to have heard of him.'

'But how are we to get there?'

'Easy – we'll take a train. There must be a train to Sligo.'

'And how are we to get to the train?'

'We'll take the bus from Enniskerry ... I'll go straight home and look at the map. And get a timetable. There's one in the kitchen!' She jumped to her feet and smiled happily. 'Now, that's all settled. Tomorrow we'll make our plans,' and getting on her bike off she cycled.

Jacko sat under the lime-tree for a long while, thinking. 'No good is going to come of this,' he said to himself. 'Mark my words.'

2

The Plan

The sun was setting like a ball of fire over Sugarloaf Mountain. Jacko stood at the tip of the long flight of steps at Enniskerry House that led down to the lake, which was guarded by two winged horses made of copper. With nostrils flaring, hooves pounding, huge wings poised for flight, he felt terror when he looked at them. Sometimes on dark winter nights he had dreams about them. He could feel their icy breath as their wings beat the air, their vicious hooves ready to strike and their terrible neigh echoing through the night. When he awoke he would tremble with fear, but it was always only the wind as it rattled his stable door.

One day he heard the story of the winged horse. The horse's name was Pegasus and his story came from Greece. Pegasus had many adventures until he arrived at the home of Zeus, the King of the Gods. There he stayed carrying lightning and thunderbolts for Zeus.

On that warm summer evening not a breath of wind ruffled the lake and Jacko thought how lucky he was to live in such a place, for his life had been hard, with many owners and much work. Behind him was the house, large and beautiful, its walls flushed pink in the setting sun, while in the gardens flowers of every colour bloomed.

As the sun set behind the mountain and the air

13

turned chill, Jacko gave a deep sigh. This plan of Fionuala's to search for her son didn't appeal to him at all. As he walked across the lawn a voice spoke close by.

'If I were you,' it said, 'I wouldn't go anywhere with that goat.'

'Who's there?' asked Jacko in alarm.

'Look up,' said the voice. 'I'm in the beech-tree.' And sure enough, sitting on a branch, was a small red squirrel.

'Who told you,' asked Jacko, 'that I'm going away?'

'The whole of County Wicklow knows,' replied the squirrel, 'that you're going with Fionuala to find her son.'

That night Jacko had a dream and it wasn't a nice one at all.

It was night in his dream and he was standing by a gloomy lake. A full moon shone down and on the water was a boat. Fionuala was rowing, but rowing in the wrong direction.

'Come back,' he yelled, 'I want to go home,' but Fionuala rowed on and disappeared from sight.

Now he was all alone. And the only way home was past those terrifying horses, whose arched legs were waiting to crush him.

He awoke with a scream. 'I'm *not* going with her to find her son,' he said to himself. 'I'll tell her today.'

As Fionuala cycled down the Long Hill, a strong wind was blowing. It buffeted her this way and that but she was so happy that she didn't notice. She reached the gates of Enniskerry House in record time only to find them locked.

'Let me in,' she bleated as she pushed and shoved, but the gates were firmly closed. There was no sign of the gate-keeper; his house was empty and quiet.

'I'll have to climb,' she thought, and climb she did.

Up, up, she went – and those gates were high. When she reached the top she paused to rest on one of the pillars.

'This is nice,' she said, as she saw the fields and the woods stretching away below her. 'That's some view!'

Having admired the view, she wanted to get down again. But the ground looked a long, long way away.

Just at that moment, a bus came round the corner. It drew to a halt and a bunch of tourists jumped out. They stared up at Fionuala as she stood on the top of the pillar and cameras clicked.

'Help!' she cried. 'Get me down!' But no one understood what she was saying.

'All in,' called the driver, as he revved up his bus.

'You'd think that goat was real,' someone said.

'Nonsense,' said another as the bus drove off. 'It was a very bad statue. Didn't look at all like a goat.'

At that moment the gate-keeper arrived. 'What are you doing up there?' he asked. 'What a strange place to be.'

He fetched a ladder and Fionuala climbed down. The gate was opened and she pushed her bike through. As she cycled off, she smiled to herself. 'I'll look good in those photos,' she thought, and she felt quite pleased.

As she arrived at the old lime-tree, Jacko was waiting. 'I'm not going with you to find your son,' he said.

'Not going,' said Fionuala and her eyes filled with tears. 'Oh, Jacko, I *couldn't* travel alone,' and she started to cry.

When Jacko saw her tears he began to weaken. 'But it's too far,' he protested. 'And we don't even know where he is!'

'We know he's in Sligo,' said Fionuala. 'Look – I've brought all my maps.'

'All right,' said Jacko. 'I'll go, but will I ever see home again?'

'Of course you will. And just think of the fun we'll have.'

And so the planning began. Day after day they studied the maps and looked at the route.

'It's quite easy,' said Fionuala. 'We go by Meath

and Westmeath and Longford and Leitrim. I wonder
could we take in Clonmacnoise? I've always wanted
to see Clonmacnoise.'

'No,' implored Jacko. 'No detours. Take the
shortest route. Why do you want to see Clonmacnoise anyway? You didn't think all that much of
Glendalough. Besides, trains don't make detours.'

'We could go by car,' said Fionuala. 'That would
be fun.'

'Who'd drive?' asked Jacko. 'Neither you nor I can
do that.'

'I'd learn,' said Fionuala. 'I'm sure I could.'

Jacko shuddered at the thought. 'I'm certainly not
going with you if you go by car.'

'All right then,' said Fionuala regretfully. 'So the
plan is: we go into Enniskerry, get the bus to Dublin,
and take the train to Sligo. Could anything be
simpler?'

'I'll tell you when – and if – we get to Sligo,' said
Jacko darkly.

At last the great day arrived. Fionuala was up early.
She had some packing to do: two carrots, a few
sprouts, some lettuce – and her hat. As she put it on
she was thinking of Jacko's hat.

One day last summer she had gone to visit him.
On the way she was plagued by flies, which buzzed
and swarmed all around her. 'Shoo . . . go away,' she
kept shouting, without much success, 'Poor Jacko,'
she thought, 'he'll be driven wild today,' for Jacko
hated flies.

But Jacko wasn't driven wild at all. He was relax-
ing comfortably under the lime-tree. 'What do you

think of this?' he asked. 'Come and look.'

Fionuala looked and began to laugh, for perched on Jacko's head was a large straw hat, with two holes for his ears. Around the brim corks were hanging. 'You can laugh,' said Jacko, 'but it keeps the flies away.' He shook his head, the corks swung, and a large bluebottle buzzed angrily away.

Fionuala thought Jacko's hat was great, and the more she thought about it the more she wanted a hat too. Then one day, as she passed the kitchen at Sugerloaf Farm, she saw, lying on the window-sill, a hat. It was an old hat with a battered brim, not the kind of hat that Fionuala fancied at all – she would have preferred a straw hat with roses – but she picked it up and put it carefully on her head. She tried to see her reflection in the glass but she couldn't see much, for the hat almost covered her eyes.

'It'll have to do,' she thought, 'until I get a nicer one.' She hid it in the goat house but she never wore it again. Now the time had come to show it to the world.

Her friend Siobhan wept as she saw Fionuala leave. 'You could come too,' said Fionuala, 'you'd enjoy the trip.'

'I couldn't,' replied Siobhan, 'I've a baby to mind,' and she looked fondly at her little kid.

On a pile of straw the cat was lying. As Fionuala approached he pretended to be asleep.

'You're a lazy cat,' said Fionuala, 'you're always asleep.'

'You're a busy-body goat,' he replied, 'and your hat looks daft.'

She went through the stable yard where she met

the brown mare who said, 'I've a sister in the west. Give her my love.'

'What's your sister called?' asked Fionuala.

'Connemara Susie,' replied the brown mare. 'She's very well known in show circles.'

As Fionuala went round the corner, Big Bill was looking out of his shed. 'So you're off,' he said. 'Don't bother to come back. And don't bring that no-good son of yours back with you either.'

'How could I bring *him* back if I didn't come back myself?' retorted Fionuala. 'But don't worry. I'll be back all right. I only hope you're gone by then.'

'And where would I go?' asked Big Bill. 'We can't all have holidays you know.'

'Maybe you'll be dead,' replied Fionuala, and she hurried on as Big Bill thumped and banged his shed door.

And so, with much waving and many good-byes, Fionuala left. Down the Long Hill she skipped, humming a happy tune, stumbling a little as her hat slipped over her eyes. Once she walked into a sleeping sheep who fled with a bleat of terror. Mist rolled over the valley and the air was damp but excitement kept Fionuala warm. On and on she went, up little hills and round twirly bends, until, just as the mist lifted and the sun peeped out, she came to the gates of Enniskerry House.

Jacko was waiting. 'What took you so long?' he said. 'I thought you'd never come.'

He grew afraid as they hurried down the hill. 'Will they let us on the bus?' he asked nervously.

In the village the bus was waiting, the engine running and the door open wide, but of the driver there was no sign.

'Quick,' said Fionuala, 'sit at the back,' and they scrambled in, just in time, as the driver appeared.

'I'm glad,' said Fionuala, 'I brought my hat,' and indeed it was a perfect disguise.

The engine roared, the brake was released, as slowly and surely the bus left Enniskerry village.

3

The Journey Begins

As the bus drove off, Fionuala bounced excitedly in her seat. 'I like this,' she said, 'this is fun.'

'Keep your voice down,' said Jacko, his eyes on the driver's back. 'Sit still,' he said over and over again.

They passed through the Scalp and came to the Country Club. On the dry ski-slope people zigzagged down.

'I could do that,' said Fionuala, 'I'd love to try.'

The bus stopped and an old man got on. He sat near Fionuala and stared at her hard. 'I'm glad to see you,' he said, 'on this bus. I've been working for Animal Rights for years.' As he left he spoke again. 'Next time I'll bring me wee pig and the wife can bring her hen.'

'That man was right,' said Fionuala, 'animals have no rights,' and before Jacko could stop her, she leaped to her feet shouting 'UP ANIMAL RIGHTS'.

'HELP!' screamed someone, 'there's a goat on this bus.'

The bus screeched to a halt and the driver left the wheel. He looked at the animals in disbelief. 'Who put these creatures on?' he roared. 'Is someone playing a joke?' and before they knew what was happening Fionuala and Jacko were out on the roadside.

As the bus moved off Fionuala banged angrily on

the door. The driver shook his fist and drove off fast.

'Another fine mess you've got us into,' said Jacko. 'Can you never hold your tongue?'

'A principle is a principle,' said Fionuala tossing her head, and picking up her luggage off she strode.

'What do we do now?' asked Jacko as he trotted behind.

'We hitch,' replied Fionuala. 'I'll be good at that.'

On the bus a row had broken out. 'Disgraceful,' said a lady, poking the driver in the back, 'turning those animals off.'

'I don't agree,' said a man. 'Putting them off was right.'

'I like animals,' said a boy who was on his way to school.

'I don't,' said another, and so the row raged, on and on.

When the driver arrived in Dublin his nerves were shattered. That evening, as he ate his supper, he told his wife about his day.

'A goat wearing a hat?' said his wife. 'On your bus?' and she looked at her husband in disbelief. 'Poor man,' she thought, 'with all that driving he's gone soft in the head,' and she hurriedly switched on TV.

On the road the animals trudged along. The traffic roared past, but although they waved and signalled not one car stopped.

'Mean creatures,' said Fionuala, 'selfish humans,' and she made some rude faces at the passing cars.

After a while they came to Kilternan National School. 'Let's go in,' said Fionuala. 'I like school.'

'Certainly not,' said Jacko and, with difficulty, he

moved her past.

On they walked until something happened, something bad. Jacko began to limp. He walked slower
and slower, as he became more and more lame.

'What's wrong?' asked Fionuala. 'Why can't you
walk?'

'I've a stone in my foot,' replied Jacko and he held
it up for Fionuala to see. Fionuala looked closely
and, sure enough, there was a stone in Jacko's foot.

'It's as big as a rock,' she said, 'quite huge.'

'Can you remove it?' asked Jacko in distress. 'Try
and knock it out.' But although Fionuala poked and
banged, the stone wouldn't budge.

'I can't walk another step,' said Jacko and he sank
down at the edge of the road.

Just then a jogger appeared. As he drew near,

Jacko called out, 'Could you help me, please? I've a stone in my foot.'

'Out of my way,' replied the jogger, not understanding a word, and he ran on faster still.

Across the road a girl was walking, a girl in smart white jeans.

'Hi,' called Fionuala. 'Could you help us please?' and she smiled a very nice smile.

The girl turned pale and began to run. 'Don't come near me,' she shrieked.

'Humans,' said Fionuala, 'are thick. They understand nothing at all.'

The road grew quiet as the traffic thinned.

'If you went to hospital,' said Fionuala, 'they'd cut off your foot. That would cure the pain.'

'I'm NOT going to hospital,' Jacko replied. 'All I need is *someone* to remove this stone.'

Along the road came a car, travelling fast. Braking suddenly, it reversed to where the animals stood.

'What's up?' called the driver. 'Are you in trouble of some kind?'

'We'll soon fix that,' he said when he saw what was wrong. Gently he lifted Jacko's foot and with a flick of a hoof-pick he removed the stone, a small one, not a huge one at all.

'You're clever,' said Fionuala. 'Who taught you that?'

'I'm a vet,' he replied, and being a vet he understood everything the animals said.

'Just what I need,' said Fionuala. 'I've an itchy nose and a tickly tongue.'

So the vet looked at her nose and examined her tongue and there was nothing wrong at all.

'Must have been my imagination,' said Fionuala. 'I've a *very* good imagination.'

'I'll say,' thought Jacko.

'Where are you off to?' asked the vet.

'We're going to Sligo,' said Fionuala. 'By train. On Very Important Business.'

The vet looked impressed. 'Hop in,' he said. 'I'll drop you at the station. But we'll have to hurry. I have a call to make.'

The car whizzed round corners and accelerated on the straight. Jacko nervously shut his eyes but Fionuala loved the speed. She leaned over the vet's shoulder, breathing in his ear, but he didn't seem to mind at all, not even when she honked the horn. At last they slowed down and turned into a farmyard. The vet grabbed his bag and left the car, with Fionuala following.

At that moment the farmer appeared, leading a large, fat bull. 'Get rid of that goat,' he roared, so Fionuala had to retreat into the car. The bull had noticed her. His small angry eyes never left her face.

'What an ugly brute,' she said. 'He'd frighten the dead.'

'Don't talk so loud,' groaned Jacko, but the bull had heard and with a roar of rage, he plunged. The farmer's sons came running to help, for the bull's temper was up.

At last the vet finished. As the farmer led the bull away, Fionuala called out, 'You're a great big bully and a nasty one, too.' It was lucky that the car was already moving, for the bull got into a towering rage.

'If you bring that goat again,' roared the farmer, 'I'll shoot her.'

The car sped along the road and Dublin drew near. As the traffic thickened, it roared and swirled. Horns blared, lights flashed, and Fionuala and Jacko were afraid. They jumped and started and trembled and shook, and even Fionuala tried to cover her eyes. When they thought they would die of fright, the car stopped at last.

'Connolly Station,' said the vet. 'What time is your train?'

'On the hour, every hour,' said Fionuala, still in a state of shock.

The vet decided to check. He went into the station and was back in a second. 'You've missed it, 'he panted, 'and there isn't another until late this evening. What will you do now?'

'We'll go home,' said Jacko. 'That's what we'll do.'

On the station wall, a large poster said:

VISIT DUBLIN ZOO

'*That's* what we'll do,' said Fionuala. 'We'll visit the zoo.'

'Well, it is a *bit* out of my way,' said the vet. 'but as I've brought you this far, I may as well go the whole hog.'

4

The Zoo

At the zoo gates the vet said good-bye. Fionuala joined the queue but Jacko hung back. 'I'm not going in,' he said, 'you'll have to go alone.'

'Why not?' asked Fionuala. 'What's wrong with you now?'

'Do you know,' asked Jacko, 'what a zoo is like?'

'Of course I do,' replied Fionuala. 'There'll be animals from the whole world.'

'Yes,' said Jacko, 'and in cages too.'

'Cages?' said Fionuala. 'Whatever do you mean?'

'You'll see,' answered Jacko darkly as he turned away.

A line of schoolgirls was waiting at the turnstile. Fionuala joined them, her hat down low over her eyes. One by one the girls filed in. The ticket-man looked up as Fionuala approached. He saw a small figure in a battered hat.

'Good morning, teacher,' he said, '*you* get in free.'

Fionuala walked along the path and her spirits rose. On a large lake ducks were swimming, while swans sailed by, their feathers ruffled by the breeze. At the water's edge pink flamingoes stood on legs like stilts.

'Jacko's wrong,' thought Fionuala, 'there are no cages here.' Then she came to some high wire-meshed enclosures. Inside monkeys jumped and played. They swung from the bars and ate bananas

and nuts. They chattered and jibbered and made faces at the crowd. When they saw Fionuala they made very rude faces indeed. Fionuala walked on, deep in thought. She came to the aviary where birds flitted and flew. They twittered and chirruped and the air was full of song.

'Silly old goat,' said a voice behind her.

'Lock her up,' said another.

Fionuala shrank in horror, expecting the worst, but it was only two parrots sitting on a perch. 'That was a bad fright,' she thought as the parrots called again.

'Mind your manners,' one said.

'Shut up, you idiot,' said the second.

'Shut up yourself,' she said and hurried out.

In the Reptile House, she tried to distinguish the snakes from the pieces of bark and tree-trunks in each cage. At that moment a roar echoed through the zoo. It rolled over the lake, died away, and then began again.

'Lions?' wondered Fionuala in great fear. 'Are they loose?' But then the roaring stopped and all was still. Fionuala had never seen lions before, so she just had to go and look. In their enclosure was a fine big male. A lioness lay in the sunshine, yawning and asleep. The male opened his mouth to roar again.

'What big teeth you've got, Grandma,' said Fionuala

The lion fixed her with a cold and angry stare. 'I'll show you what my teeth can do,' he shouted and picking up a joint of meat he bit it clean in two.

'Show-off,' called Fionuala but she quickly moved on.

Not far away was the polar bear. He was having a swim. Backwards and forwards he swam as the water rushed and flowed.

'You'll get a cold,' called Fionuala, 'if you stay in too long.'

'Is that so?' replied the bear and he swam faster still.

'You're very pale,' called Fionuala. 'You look frozen to me.'

'Shove off,' said the bear

'I've thought of a poem,' said Fionuala. 'Would you like to hear it?'

'Take a walk,' growled the bear, but Fionuala said it anyway:

Fuzzy wuzzy was a wuzzy,
Fuzzy wuzzy was a bear.
Fuzzy wuzzy was a wuzzy,
Fuzzy wuzzy lost his hair

And she disappeared fast.

On the lawn a crowd was gathered, laughing and in a happy mood. Fionuala edged forward, trying to see. A photocall was taking place with three chimpanzees, one a baby.

'Look this way, Lucy,' called the keeper to the baby chimp but she wouldn't, for Lucy was being bold. She threw food at the crowd and rubbed it in her hair. Everyone laughed but the keeper was not amused. Picking Lucy up he took her away. Fionuala followed. She watched as the keeper opened a door, closed it again, and disappeared. Fionuala peeped in.

'Hello,' she said, 'would you like to play?'

'Go walkie,' said Lucy jumping up.

So Fionuala opened the cage door – and it wasn't hard – and she lifted Lucy out. The little creature kissed her with a large wet kiss. She reached for Fionuala's hat and threw it in the air.

'Naughty,' scolded Fionuala but she really didn't mind.

Standing in a corner was a push-chair, all shiny and new, and Fionuala tucked the baby in. Now Fionuala hadn't wheeled a push-chair before, so first she went too fast and then she went too slow, but soon she got the pace just right.

People smiled as they passed. 'Isn't it marvellous,' they said, 'what animals can do.' As they walked, Lucy talked her baby talk, for she was just learning

to speak. 'Tee tocks,' she said, pointing to the peacocks on the lawn. 'Gas,' and she looked at the rich green grass. She sang a little song but Fionuala couldn't make head or tail of it at all.

They passed the zebras and came to the giraffes.

'Necky,' said Lucy pointing to one.

'That's a good name for a giraffe,' thought Fionuala and she called out, 'Hi, Necky.'

The giraffe stopped eating and with slow, dainty steps approached. Stretching out her neck, she looked Fionuala in the eye. 'Insults,' she said, 'I do not like. My name is BECKY.'

On they went and they heard the camels groan.

'Dook and Dommy,' said Lucy as the camels approached.

'Who are you?' asked the camels, looking Fionuala up and down.

'And I'm Fionuala,' she replied proudly. 'The Glendalough goat.'

'Never heard of you,' said the camels.

'I've never heard of *you*,' answered Fionuala. 'Dook and Dommy indeed! Why do you have such weird names?'

'Can't you read?' shouted the camels, pointing to a notice on the wall. 'These camels,' it said, 'are called Duke and Tommy.'

'I think,' said Fionuala, 'that it's time to take you home, Lucy.'

At that moment keepers came running up.

'Catch that goat,' they shouted, 'she's stolen the baby chimpanzee.'

Across the zoo Fionuala tore, past the cages and the lake, and as she ran her hat took wing. It sailed over the tree-tops and the lawn, and landed with a 'plop' right on the elephant's head.

As she rushed out through the zoo gate Jacko was waiting. 'You stayed too long,' he said, 'we've missed that evening train,' and he was very upset indeed. But Fionuala ran on. 'Come back,' he shouted but she wouldn't. On and on she ran, with Jacko panting behind.

5

Nightmares

'What happened?' asked Jacko, when he finally caught up with Fionuala. 'Did they put you in a cage?'

'Certainly not,' answered Fionuala. 'I had a very nice time.'

They reached the main road and the traffic boomed by.

'I can see grass,' said Fionuala. 'Perhaps it's a park,' and it was.

In the Phoenix Park the grass was soft and the trees were shady, and before long the animals were asleep. When they awoke it was almost dark. Their tummies rumbled as they began to graze. Amongst the trees, dark figures stood watching.

'Are they friend or foe?' those figures asked each other, as silently they crept up.

Jacko was grazing but Fionuala stopped. She raised her head and looked around. On all sides large animals surrounded them. 'Jacko,' she whispered in a shaky voice, 'we're going to be attacked.'

They waited, hearts thumping, eyes closed, for the attack. But it never came.

The herd of deer peered through the gloom and they began to laugh. 'It's a poor old donkey,' they said, 'and a batty goat.'

And so night fell and the deer were kind. They showed where the sweetest grass grew and the freshest stream tumbled. When the herd lay down to rest, Fionuala and Jacko lay down too, but they found it hard to sleep.

'Jacko,' whispered Fionuala, 'I want to ask you. Why do you hate zoos?'

'Because animals are kept in cages,' said Jacko.

'But they seemed so happy today.'

'How do you know? Did you talk to them?'

'Well, only the odd remark . . . ' began Fionuala as Jacko interrupted, 'How would *you* like to be shut up in cage all your life? Not being able to run around. Or gallop. Or kick your heels up. Our lives may be hard but theirs must be terrible.'

'But there are zoos where the animals can roam around.' Seeing that Jacko was still looking depressed, she added, 'Zoos may be bad but at least the animals are safe. If they were in their own countries, they would probably be killed by other animals or humans.'

'I know.' Jacko gave a great sigh. 'That's what makes it so difficult. I don't know what to think. All I know is that to be free is the most important thing in life.'

'Well we're not going to solve these problems' said Fionuala. 'Now, we'd better go to sleep.'

Eventually they slept, and at dawn, before they were awake, the deer left as silently as they had come.

Fionuala and Jacko hurried from the park, past the President's house with sentries at the gate, past the zoo where they heard the lions roar. They trotted along the quays, over O'Connell Bridge and along by the Custom House and the river Liffey, until they

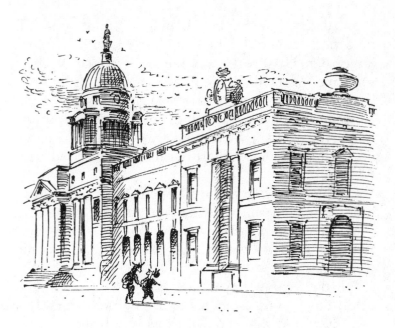

came to Connolly Station. There was no traffic on the roads at all. The station was empty, too, except for the Sligo train. They tried to open a few doors.

'They're all locked,' said Jacko. But luckily one was open. Wearily they climbed in. They fell asleep immediately and they both dreamed dreams.

In Fionuala's dream she was in a dark spooky wood. Above the tree-tops the sky was full of stars. She was walking fast but something was following. She could hear feet coming nearer and nearer still. Suddenly a star fell, down, down to the earth below and the wood was full of its light. A voice began to sing and Fionuala heard again that strange song that Lucy the baby chimp sang.

At the end of the song, a lion roared, 'What are you singing? Sing the right words or you're a goner.'

Fionuala tried to sing but though her mouth opened no sound came out. The lion charged, with an extra large roar. His breath was hot on her face. With a scream of terror she woke up.

In Jacko's dream he was in a garden full of flowers. A stream tumbled by and in the distance were purple hills. He was happy and content – until he saw the horse. It was galloping fast but its feet never touched the ground.

'The winged horse,' he whispered and he tried to hide. Through the trees he ran but the horse ran faster. Too late he saw what his fate was to be, for right in his path was a large black cage. Then he woke up.

'I had a terrible dream,' he said.

'So did I,' said Fionuala and they both trembled with fright. At that moment a whistle blew and the

train lurched forward

'This is nice,' said Fionuala happily, as it gathered speed. 'This is really nice,' she said, as she put her luggage on the rack. She looked out of the window at the houses and the shops. She watched the cars and the buses as they passed them by. Soon the city disappeared and green fields came in sight. She saw horses and cows and sheep and pigs. On and on the train went.

'Did you bring food?' she asked Jacko. 'Have you anything to eat?'

Jacko opened his bag. He had brought cabbage and hay and apples. They shared the food and munched away happily. But someone was coming! Down the carriage came the guard and he was very angry indeed.

'OUT!' he roared. 'It's the luggage van for you. Out! OUT! OUT!'

The train had stopped at a small station and, with loud protests and angry words, he bundled them out on to the platform and into an enclosed van.

'Animal Rights,' shouted Fionuala as the door banged shut. She kicked and thumped the van walls as the train thundered on. 'You're wasting your time,' said a voice close by. 'They won't let you out, you know.'

'Who's there?' asked Fionuala, peering around.

'Look behind you,' replied the voice.

Fionuala looked and there, staring through the bars of a box, was a large pigeon.

'That's a terrible way to travel,' she said. 'Shut up like that.'

'I like it,' replied the bird. 'I'm resting before my

race.' As they talked something rustled in the corner.

'Who's that?' asked Fionuala. 'Is someone there?'

'It's the train mouse,' whispered the pigeon. 'He's always on the move.'

'What class of a mouse is that?' asked Fionuala. 'Sounds daft to me.'

'Not as daft as you,' said the mouse coming close.

Fionuala looked at the mouse and she didn't like what she saw.

'I hate country animals,' said the mouse. 'I'm a townee myself.'

'I dislike town creatures,' replied Fionuala. 'They smell of soot and smoke.'

And as their talk went on and on the insults flew.

'When do we get to Sligo?' asked Fionuala. 'How long does it take?'

'You're not a great traveller, are you?' sneered the mouse, 'I've been everywhere myself.'

'How stupid,' said Fionuala, 'to keep travelling all the time'

The mouse leaped with rage and landed on Fionuala's back.

'GET OFF,' she howled but the mouse clung tight. 'Let me out,' she screamed as the train began to slow. It clanked over the tracks and with a jolt it stopped. The door opened as the mouse fled. Fionuala hurtled on to the platform, knocking people to right and left, and rushed out through the entrance gates.

As she slowed down, Jacko came panting up.

'Fionuala,' he said, 'we've made a terrible mistake. This isn't Sligo at all.'

'Not Sligo?' she replied. 'Whatever do you mean?'

In horror she followed Jacko's gaze. By the roadside was a sign and on it were the words:

WELCOME TO MULLINGAR

The train gave two mocking hoots as, with much noise, it left to continue its journey to Sligo.

'Another fine mess you've got us into,' said Jacko.

Fionuala tossed her head. 'I'm not going to let a little thing like this get in my way. Come on! We'll find some way of getting to Sligo. It can't be all that far.'

6
Nooly

Mullingar was quite deserted as Fionuala and Jacko walked through the streets, so there were few people around to stare at the odd couple.

Fionuala stopped in front of a china shop. She could hardly believe her eyes. There, sitting in the middle of the cups and saucers and plates, was a dog, a brown and white dog with amber-coloured eyes. She looked at Fionuala and her tail began to wag. As it wagged a plate crashed to the floor.

'GET OUT,' a man's voice roared, 'AND DON'T COME BACK,' and he threw her out through the door, right at Fionuala's feet.

'Hello,' said the dog, 'I'm Nooly. Who are you?'

At that moment the shopkeeper appeared. When he saw a donkey and a goat he gave a gasp.

'There's a zoo outside,' he yelled, and retreating inside he locked the door and pulled down all the blinds.

Up the street the animals went, Fionuala and Nooly chatting happily. Jacko, lagging behind, didn't speak.

'What's wrong?' asked Fionuala. 'Why won't you talk?'

'I dislike dogs,' replied Jacko. 'You know that well.'

'But this dog is nice,' said Fionuala. 'She's already my friend.'

As they left the town behind, Nooly bounced and jumped, wanting to play.

'Stop it,' said Jacko, 'I've had enough of you.'

At Jacko's words, Nooly's head hung low and tears slid down her face.

'You're a fine one!' said Fionuala angrily. 'All this talk about being kind to animals! And look at how you've upset this poor dog!'

'I'm sorry,' said Jacko humbly. 'What's wrong with her? Why does she cry?'

So Nooly told her tale and it was a sad one indeed.

'One day,' she said, 'I was with Freddie, my friend. We played a game of chase and it was fun. Then a van arrived and a man put me inside. Off we drove fast but I wanted to go home. "You're going to a new one now," said the man and he drove faster still. At last we arrived and I didn't like that home at

all. They took off my collar and shut me in a shed. I was cold and hungry and afraid. In the morning a boy came and I thought we would play but he hit me with stones and a great big stick.'

'How did you escape?' asked Fionuala, 'and get to Mullingar?'

'I dug a hole in the shed,' replied Nooly, 'and then I ran away.'

'Why were you in the china shop?' asked Fionuala. 'That was a strange place to be.'

'I was cold and tired,' replied Nooly. 'I wanted to sleep.'

'I'm tired now,' said Jacko. So they went into a field and were soon asleep.

As the animals slept, a fox walked by and a hedgehog rustled in the bushes. A full moon turned the world to silver as an owl called.

With the first streaks of dawn Nooly awoke. She yawned and stretched, and with her brown nose to the ground she began to hunt. This way and that way she ran, chasing the rabbits before her.

Once more the animals took to the road. Suddenly, a van came round the corner. As it drew near, Nooly shivered with fear.

'It's that man,' she whimpered, 'the one who took me away,' but it wasn't, for the van sped on. The animals grew uneasy at every passing car.

'Let's take to the fields,' said Jacko, 'it's safer there.' But the fields were full of cows.

And so the day passed. Nooly was silent, her amber eyes sad. As darkness came rain began to fall. The animals huddled as thunder crashed. A flash of lightning turned the night to day and Fionuala saw a dark object close by.

'That's a tractor,' she thought, 'we could shelter there.'

The tractor was old but it was warm and dry and the animals felt safe. The storm passed and the morning sun shone. Fionuala wakened first. 'This tractor is nice,' she thought as she looked around. She peered in the mirror, turning her head this way and that. She admired the steering-wheel and the gears and the brake. And then she saw something else! The key was in the ignition, just waiting to be turned. She turned it and the engine sprang to life.

Nooly and Jacko wakened as the tractor began to move. 'Are we going for a drive?' asked Nooly. 'That's nice.'

'STOP!' shrieked Jacko, but it was too late. They were already moving.

Fionuala steered carefully as she tried the gears and the brakes and they jerked along. Jacko scolded and pleaded, and then sank back moaning, for Fionuala wouldn't stop. They met a milk van and Fionuala waved. The van wobbled and nearly hit the verge. A motor-cyclist drew level and then swerved and nearly crashed.

But something was wrong. The engine spluttered and coughed and finally died. The petrol tank was empty. As the tractor rolled to a halt Jacko opened his eyes. Wrenching open the door he leaped out.

'What a pity,' said Fionuala, 'that was fun,' and Nooly agreed.

On they walked, trying to hitch, but not one car stopped. Then something happened and it was very frightening indeed. A police van appeared and drew to a halt. The window was opened and a young man looked out.

'Animals on the road,' he said. 'We can't have that!' He loaded them into the van.

'Where are they taking us?' wondered Fionuala, very alarmed.

'With what are we charged?' whispered Jacko, much afraid. But Nooly liked the ride.

Along the road they sped and Longford drew near. At the Garda Station the car stopped.

'Come and see this?' called their driver as the sergeant appeared.

'It's the Pound for them,' he said, 'that's where they'll go.'

In the Garda Station people stared in amazement as the animals came in. But Fionuala had had enough. She charged at the sergeant, lifting him off his feet. She turned over tables and chairs and desks. The guards ran in all directions, pushing and shoving to get out.

'Lock the door,' they shouted, 'those animals are wild.'

'You know,' said Jacko, 'what will happen now. We'll be locked up for life!'

But something was happening outside. A blue car arrived and two people jumped out. Voices sounded, all talking together. The door opened and Nooly's owners ran in. What a joyful reunion took place! 'We've been searching for days,' they said. 'The mountains, the valleys, the sea, everywhere.'

It was time to say good-bye.

'These animals,' said Nooly's owners, 'seem to be her friends. What will happen to them now?'

'It's the Pound for them,' said the sergeant. 'That goat is completely wild.'

'She looks gentle to us,' they answered. 'She'd make a lovely pet.'

'I've a sister in Limerick,' a young guard said. 'She'd give these animals a home.' And so it was all arranged.

'Where's Limerick?' asked Jacko when Nooly had gone. 'Is it near Sligo, do you know?'

'I'm sure it is,' replied Fionuala. 'Just down the road,' and she smiled her happy smile. As they waited for their transport she was excited.

'I hope,' she said, 'that we travel in style. A BMW or a Jag would be nice.' But when their transport arrived it wasn't stylish at all.

7

Puck Fair

Outside the Garda Station a truck was waiting. From inside came the sound of banging, as the animals moved around. The ramp was lowered and a strong bullock smell flowed out. Fionuala looked in horror at their large muscular backs.

'I can't go in there,' she cried, 'I'll be trampled to death,' and she tried to run. Strong hands held her back and they pushed her in. Jacko followed.

'Help!' she screamed but the sound came out as a long, long 'ba-a-a-a-a-a'. Jacko didn't protest; he had travelled with bullocks before.

The ramp was shut, the engine started, and away to Limerick they went. Fionuala felt dizzy and her legs felt weak. She leaned against Jacko with her eyes closed tight.

'Are you all right?' asked a voice beside her. 'Have you enough room?'

Fionuala opened her eyes and returned the bullock's gentle stare. With her courage returning, she began to speak and soon she and the bullock were friends.

'Can you tell jokes?' she asked him. 'That would be fun.' He nodded.

'What would you get,' he asked, 'if you blew down a rabbit hole?'

'Let me guess,' she said, but she didn't know the answer.

'Hot cross bunnies,' replied the bullock and all the animals laughed.

'Do you know any more?' asked Fionuala.

'I do,' replied the bullock. 'What happens when vampires get together?' Everyone looked blank. 'They drive each other batty.'

'What happens when you phone a bee?' put in another bullock. And before anyone could answer he said, 'You get a buzzy line.'

'Where do frogs leave their hats?' said the gentle bullock. There was silence all around. 'In the croak-room.'

'Now it's my turn,' said Fionuala. 'What happened when the girl in the dairy met a goat?'

'What?' shouted all the bullocks.

'He turned to butt-her,' answered Fionuala. 'Here's another: when is it unlucky to see a black cat?'

'When?' asked the bullocks.

'When you're a mouse,' replied Fionuala.

'They're pretty feeble,' scoffed Jacko. 'Don't you know any good human jokes?'

'No, do you?' asked Fionuala.

'Of course I do: how do you confuse a man on a building site?' Everyone thought hard so Jacko answered, 'Line up five shovels and tell him to take his pick!'

'I know another one,' said the smallest bullock. 'One human says to another, "Guess how many piglets I have in this bag and you can have both of them?"'

'That's not a joke,' objected Fionuala, 'Didn't he tell him how many piglets there were?'

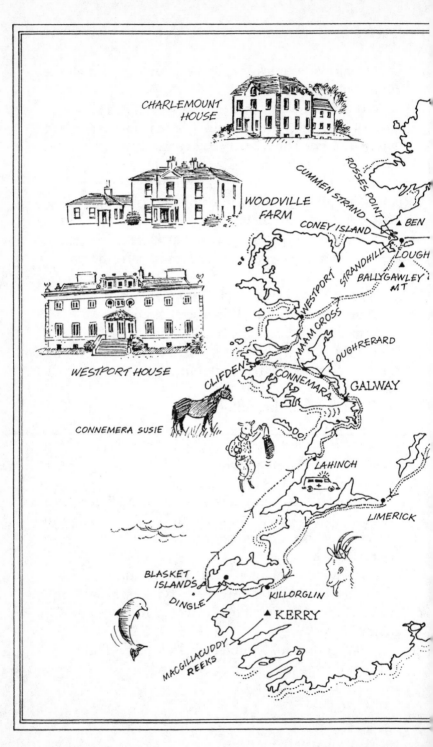

CHARLEMOUNT HOUSE

WOODVILLE FARM

WESTPORT HOUSE

CONNEMERA SUSIE

ROSSES POINT

CUMMEN STRAND

CONEY ISLAND

▲ BEN

STRANDHILL

LOUGH

▲

BALLYGAWLEY MT

WESTPORT

MAAM CROSS

OUGHRERARD

CLIFDEN

CONNEMARA

GALWAY

LAHINCH

LIMERICK

BLASKET ISLANDS

DINGLE

KILLORGLIN

▲ KERRY

MACGILLACUDDY REEKS

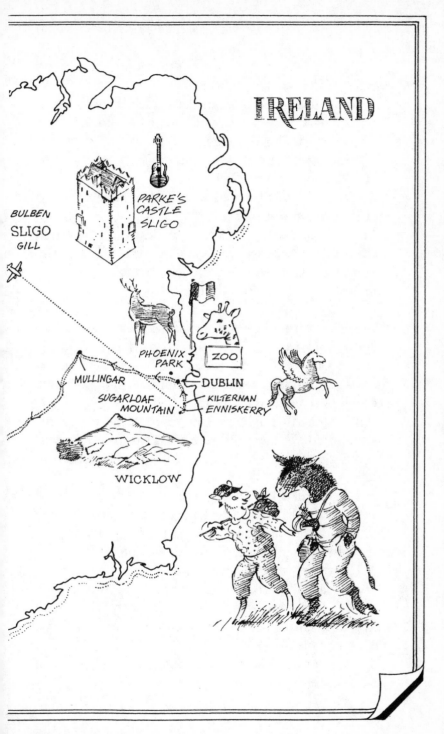

'Ah, but it is. Guess what the second man answered? He said, "Is it three?"'

And so the miles passed. As Limerick drew near, Fionuala asked, 'Where would goats be found?'

'At Shannon,' said the gentle bullock.'

'At Listowel,' shouted another.

'Or Ballybunion or Tralee.'

Every bullock had a different idea. They argued and shouted and disagreed.

'You're all wrong,' said the smallest bullock, when all the others paused to draw breath. 'I know the very place. Killorglin. That's where they have Puck Fair.' And every bullock agreed.

When at last they arrived in Limerick, darkness had fallen. The ramp was lowered and the animals climbed out, stiff and tired, but glad to be free. In the fuss and bustle, Jacko and Fionuala slipped away. No one noticed as they disappeared.

They went through the town and came to a signpost marked: *To Kerry*. 'We're on the right road,' said Fionuala happily. They stopped to graze and then to sleep.

They were up with the sun next morning and walking along the road when a van pulled up beside them. It rattled and banged as it rolled to a stop, the engine belching smoke. Two men got out.

''Tis water we need,' said one.

'Aye,' said the other. Then they saw Fionuala.

'What have we here?' they said with winks and nods, 'and an old ass, too. Come on, me darlings, we'll take you to Puck Fair.'

It was dark in the van but Fionuala was pleased.

'What luck!' she said. 'We're going to Puck Fair.'
But Jacko was deep in thought.

It was a very uncomfortable journey. The van
shook and rocked from side to side. Fumes belched
from the exhaust and came up through the floor
boards. And every time the driver put on the brakes,
there was a grinding, ear-splitting noise. As mile
followed mile, Fionuala coughed and spluttered,
longing for air.

At last they stopped. Roughly they were dragged
out and ropes were put around their necks. Fionuala
hadn't expected that at all.

'Jacko,' she bleated, but Jacko had disappeared. In
terror she bucked and kicked and jumped.

'You've a wild one there,' someone said. 'How
much do you want for her?'

At those terrible words Fionuala fainted.

When she came to, she was tied to a wall with Jacko beside her. 'I thought,' she said, with tears flowing, 'I'd never see you again.'

As the animals stood with bowed heads, something was happening. Musicians came down the street and with them was a goat, pure white with a proud head, as handsome a goat as you ever saw. People parted to let him pass. On to a platform he was hoisted, high above the crowd.

'All hail for King Puck,' a man shouted, placing a crown on the goat's head and the crowd went wild.

'Is it Daniel?' Jacko whispered and his voice shook.

'No,' replied Fionuala, 'but I thought it was,' and her tears flowed again.

High on his platform King Puck surveyed the crowd. He looked over the people and he saw a goat, a white goat, tied to a wall.

He looked and he looked again, and he couldn't believe what he saw.

'Fionuala,' he called down, 'it's me, Patrick Cool-Boy, your cousin,' and with a great leap he was down on the ground.

Pandemonium broke out as people scattered. In a second Patrick had untied both Fionuala and Jacko.

'Follow me,' he shouted. And they did.

8

By Boat to Lahinch

Through the crowded Killorglin streets ran Patrick, with Fionuala and Jacko following close behind. They crossed the bridge at the end of the hill, and as they left the town behind their pace slowed. Now they could talk and, as they walked along, there was much to say.

'I recognised you at once,' said Patrick, 'but you didn't know me.'

'You were only a baby when we last met,' said Fionuala, and she remembered her journey to Glendalough and her relations, the Cool-Boys. 'How is Auntie Bridget?'

'She's well,' replied Patrick, 'and the girls too.'

And Fionuala remembered her cousins – Maureen and Carmel and Mary and Fidelma and Oonah and Aoife and Leila and Grainne and Niamh and Cara and the twins Ailish and Eilish. What a wild lot they were.

'And Kevin,' said Fionuala, 'how is he?'

'Kevin's the reason,' Patrick answered, 'that I left Glendalough. Bossing me here and bossing me there, telling me what to do and how to do it all day long. I couldn't stand it another minute, so I packed my bags and left.'

'What brought you here?' asked Fionuala. 'You're a long way from home.'

'I kept travelling,' replied Patrick, 'until I found

the MacGillacuddy Reeks. I liked them so there I stayed.'

'You must be proud to be crowned King Puck,' said Fionuala. 'My father was King Puck, too, many years ago.'

'I'm proud indeed,' replied Patrick. 'The men came to the mountains to find a brave, strong, true Irish goat, and they chose me.'

'Being brave and strong runs in families,' replied Fionuala, 'and prettiness too,' and she smiled to herself. 'Your mother must miss you,' she said and suddenly her face clouded over, 'for I miss my son.' She told Patrick about their search for Daniel.

Patrick grew thoughtful and then he suggested a plan. 'We'll go to Lahinch. Goats live there.'

'Is Lahinch in Sligo?' asked Fionuala. 'I hope it is.'

'It's in County Clare,' replied Patrick. 'We'll go by boat.'

'I like the sea,' said Jacko. 'I swim well.'

'I can't,' wailed Fionuala, much afraid.

The sea was not very far away and there on the shore they found a boat. As Fionuala boarded she tottered and tripped. 'I'm sure we'll drown,' she moaned.

The ropes were untied and the engine hummed.

'Casting off,' called Patrick and away they went. The boat rose and fell with a gentle swish as waves tumbled and the sea slid by. Above, the sky was blue, with clouds racing and sea-birds calling, but Fionuala refused to look. Her eyes were shut tight.

'You're missing it all,' said Jacko, 'It's such a shame.'

'Just let me get on to dry land again,' said Fionuala. 'That's all I ask.'

As they approached Dingle, Fungie the dolphin appeared. He leaped and dived, circling the boat. 'Hi!' he called with a happy smile. Fionuala opened her eyes and looked. When she saw Fungie she forgot to be afraid.

'You're clever,' she called, as she watched him circling and swimming and diving. She leaned over the water and as her eyes met his she felt calm and still.

'With Fungie,' she thought, as the boat travelled on, 'I'd learn to swim. I'll come back here some day.'

The Blasket Islands came into view. Sea-birds were soaring all around the rocky peaks. Gannets flew high before plunging downwards in an amazing dive.

'Odd birds,' said Patrick. 'Soon after they're hatched they weigh more than an adult. They can only swim at first. Then they learn to dive.'

'You know so much,' said Fionuala. 'Where did you learn it all?'

'Nothing to it,' said Patrick. 'Keep your eyes and ears open. That's all.'

'I'll become an expert too,' said Fionuala.

'A pity you can't see the new centre there,' said Patrick, nodding towards land. 'There are stones outside that say: "Dúirt sé go mb'fhearr dom scríobh fad is a bheinn beo CHUN GO MBEINN BEO IS MÉ MARBH."'

'And what's that when it's at home?' said Jacko.

'Some man who lived here said it,' replied Patrick. 'It means: "He told me that I should write during my lifetime so THAT I MIGHT LIVE AFTER MY DEATH."'

'That's beautiful,' said Fionuala. 'I'll take up writing when I get back home.'

'I thought you were going to learn to swim,' said Jacko crossly. He was beginning to feel seasick. They were now in the open sea and it became very rough indeed. Fionuala stopped thinking about sea-birds and swimming and writing and shut her eyes once more. Jacko sat and suffered, watching the waves break over the bow of the boat.

Only Patrick was unconcerned. 'Nothing as healthy as a good blow,' he said and began singing sea shanties. 'Oh, for a life on the ocean wave,' he roared.

All through the day they travelled. They saw seals and puffins, razorbills and sharks. Big waves splashed them and often they got wet.

As they rounded Spanish Point something very

frightening happened. From the direction of the setting sun, a helicopter appeared like some dark monster. It flew over their boat with blades whirring and hovered, coming lower and lower still. They could even see the pilot and someone at the open door.

'What's wrong?' gasped Fionuala. 'What did we do?'

'We stole this boat,' replied Jacko. 'We'll get prison for that.'

'We didn't steal it,' said Patrick. 'We borrowed it for a day.'

'We'll all be shot,' wept Fionuala. 'I know we will.'

But suddenly the helicopter left.

'I think,' said Patrick, 'we'll go ashore for tonight. We'll travel on tomorrow.'

With skill and care he guided the boat ashore, dropping anchor by the rocks. 'There's a cave here,' he said, leading the way over the sands. Inside the cave was damp. Water dripped from the walls and ran across the floor.

'This isn't very nice,' said Fionuala, stepping daintily over the rivulets.

'Prison would be worse,' said Jacko.

The sun dipped over the horizon and the sky grew dark. Waves beat on the rocks and rolled on to the shore. Through the cave entrance they saw the stars. While they fell into an exhausted sleep, the moon rose with a cold, clear light.

Sometime during the night, Fionuala suddenly awoke.

'What was that?' she whispered. Her heart was

hammering and jumping. 'I thought I heard a noise.'

Patrick and Jacko were also awake. 'There *is* a noise,' said Patrick. 'There it is again. It's the sound of a boat engine. It's coming in to shore.'

Now they heard voices, low and clear. At the water's edge, dark figures stood and torch-light flashed.

'It's the guards,' groaned Jacko. 'I knew they'd come.'

'It's pirates,' said Fionuala, and her teeth chattered with fear. 'I can see their flag.'

'Don't make a noise,' breathed Patrick. 'Stay quite still.'

Footsteps crunched on the shingle beach. They stopped outside the cave, as the torch-light flickered and went out. Voices muttered and swore and then, panting hard, people came into the cave.

Fionuala stopped breathing and her heart stopped beating. Her lungs were bursting and her head felt light. Before she could stop herself she uttered a terrible cry. It echoed round and round the cave, like a howling, screaming ghost.

'The BANSHEE!' cried the intruders, and they ran off in terror, stumbling to get out.

With full throttle and engine roaring the boat disappeared from sight.

'Keep still,' said Patrick in a low voice. 'They may come back.'

So the animals sat as still as mice, not even talking to each other. Slowly the stars faded, the dawn broke and the cave was filled with light.

'Were they pirates?' asked Fionuala, still afraid.

'Smugglers, or thieves,' replied Patrick. 'And there's their loot.' He pointed to a box on the floor.

'Is it diamonds?' she asked hopefully. 'Or silver, or gold?'

'Let's see,' said Patrick and he lifted the lid.

But it wasn't diamonds or silver or gold. Just a few rolls of canvas. He unrolled one. It was a painting of a lady standing by a strange-looking piano.

'Junk,' said Jacko in disgust.

'No, it's pretty,' said Fionuala, thinking to herself how impressive it would look on the goat-house wall. 'I'll take it with me. We'll hide the rest away and leave the box.'

So they hid the rolls in another cave, high above the tide.

They pushed out their boat again and on they travelled, with the western sun in their eyes and salt on their lips, until they came to Lahinch. The engines were cut. Jacko jumped ashore and made fast the boat.

As Fionuala scrambled out she rocked and swayed as she walked.

'You need to get your sea legs,' joked Patrick.

'No thanks!' Fionuala tossed her head. 'I'm quite happy with them as they are.'

As they came to the road they passed a litter box. Inside was a strong plastic bag, with a drawstring top.

'Just what I need,' thought Fionuala. 'I'll put the painting inside and I'll carry it on my back.'

At Lahinch golf course, goats were standing about in clusters. They watched as the three animals drew near.

'Is there a Daniel here?' called Patrick. 'Is there any goat by that name?' But the goats shook their heads.

At that moment there was a shout of 'FORE'. A small white ball hurtled through the air and hit Jacko a terrible clout. Down he fell and lay quite still.

'He's been killed,' shrieked Fionuala, and she began to sob wildly. The goats crowded round in horror to see if he was dead.

A man and a boy came running up. 'Lor, Da,' said the boy, 'you've killed the ass.' His father's face went white.

'Get the vet,' he said and the boy ran off.

The vet came quickly, looked grave, and did a quick examination. Jacko didn't stir.

'We'll send him to Galway,' said the vet. 'He must

have his head X-rayed.'

Fionuala wept as a horse-box arrived and they carried Jacko into it. She was still weeping as she climbed in too. Patrick stood watching, with a sad unhappy face.

'I'd come with you,' he said, 'but I must return the boat.'

So Fionuala and he said their good-byes and promised to keep in touch.

As the horse-box moved, Jacko stirred. He groaned a little and moaned a little, then he sat up. 'Where am I?' he asked.

'You're alive!' cried Fionuala. 'I thought you were dead.'

'Dead?' said Jacko, puzzled. 'I never felt better,' and up he stood, as good as new.

'Where are we going?' he repeated mile after mile, but Fionuala wouldn't say.

As Galway drew near Jacko became more insistent. 'If you don't tell me,' he shouted, 'I'll wreck the horse-box. And then we'll certainly end up in jail.'

'You're going to hospital,' Fionuala explained, 'to make your head new.'

At those words, he gave a scream. 'I don't want a new head,' he bellowed. 'I like the one I've got,' and he became very wild indeed. He kicked and shouted and screamed to get out.

The horse-box stopped and the driver appeared. 'The ass has lost his head,' he said. 'We'll have to let him free.' He lowered the ramp, and before you could wink Jacko was gone. He galloped along the road in a cloud of dust and disappeared into the night.

9

Galway

When Fionuala caught up with Jacko she found him sitting on a low stone wall, staring into space. Below them the lights of Galway were beginning to twinkle in the dusk.

'How could you?' said Jacko. 'How could you do that to me?'

'Do what?' asked Fionuala. 'What do you mean?'

'Let them cut off my head,' replied Jacko. 'I thought you were my friend.'

'You've got it all wrong,' said Fionuala, and she tried to explain.

'Hit by a golf ball?' said Jacko. 'I *never* was.' And no matter what Fionuala said he didn't believe it. The whole event seemed to have been blotted from his mind.

'I hope it's not concussion,' thought Fionuala, but aloud all she said was, 'We may as well see what Galway is like as we're here.'

So on they walked towards the beckoning lights and in a little while they heard music and noise and a fairground came into view.

'How exciting – just look at that!' said Fionuala. 'Let's go,' and they did.

First they tried the switch-back, swooping up and thundering down. 'Whe-e-e!' shouted Fionuala but Jacko was afraid.

'Let me out,' he gasped as they came to a stop,

and he staggered off and nearly fell.

'Is it your head?' asked Fionuala. 'Does it hurt?'

'There's nothing wrong with my head,' he shouted, much annoyed.

Next they tried the bumper cars and Fionuala drove. 'WHAM!' she shouted as she rammed car after car.

'STOP,' roared Jacko but she wouldn't.

'Now for the Big Wheel,' said Fionuala, but Jacko refused.

'I've done enough,' he said, 'I won't do anything more.'

As the wheel began to turn, Fionuala ran towards it. With a leap and a bound she tumbled in. 'Jacko,' she called, 'watch this,' and she stood up to wave.

'Sit down,' roared everyone, 'you'll have us all killed.' But the wheel had stopped.

'There's a goat on the wheel,' voices called. 'Catch her quick.' But Fionuala had gone. She tore out of the fairground. Jacko ran after her and they never stopped until they reached Eyre Square.

Young people were standing around the statue of a man with a pushed-back cap, and there was laughter and chat on the night air. Not wanting to be seen the animals slipped into the shadows. As the moon rose and the clock struck twelve the square was quiet at last.

When the animals awoke in the early morning the air was damp but the grass in the square was sweet. They grazed a little and then wandered through the streets, stopping at Kenny's Bookshop. In the Gallery at the back, a poster caught Fionuala's eye.

'Look at that,' she said, 'there's an Art Festival

here,' and she read the poster through. 'Paint a Picture,' it said, 'and win a prize.'

'I could do that,' she said, 'I'm sure I could.'

All that day she painted. She painted the Wicklow mountains and the Glendalough lakes. And then she painted her son Daniel. At last, hot and tired, she laid down her brush, signed her picture 'Fionuala', and left it at the Gallery door.

'What about Sligo?' asked Jacko. 'Shouldn't we be on our way?'

'Soon,' replied Fionuala, 'but I want my prize first.'

They came to a travel agents and in the window was a map. 'Now,' said Fionuala looking closely, 'I'm sure Sligo is near.' But it wasn't near at all.

'I'd no idea,' replied Jacko, quite fed up, 'that the

shortest way to Sligo was via Killorglin, Lahinch and Galway. Are we going to travel all round Ireland to find your silly son?'

It was the nearest they had ever come to a quarrel. 'I'm sorry,' said Fionuala contritely. 'I know we've travelled a lot, but I would have never forgiven myself if Daniel had been at Puck Fair or on the golf course.' As tears welled in her eyes Jacko forgave her.

'All right, we'll stay for the art results,' he said. 'But after this, no more stops.'

'It's only an extra day,' said Fionuala, 'and I know I've won.'

As they waited for the painting results, they wandered here and there through the city. When they were at the quayside watching the boats, a radio blared out.

'I like that music,' said Fionuala and she began to dance.

'I want to hear the news,' replied Jacko but Fionuala had fallen asleep.

When she awoke, Jacko was looking at the sky. 'It's going to rain tonight, at eight o'clock,' he said.

Fionuala looked at the sky and she looked at the sun. 'You're wrong,' she said. But Jacko was right, for at eight o'clock *exactly*, the rain began to fall.

'How,' wondered Fionuala, 'did he know the exact time it would rain? Perhaps he can tell the future,' and she was most impressed.

Once a fortune-teller came to Sugarloaf Farm. She had a nice little tent and a lovely crystal ball and Fionuala longed to know what her future would hold. She stood watching as people went in and out but when she saw the farmer's wife approaching, she followed. Outside the little tent she leaned close and what she heard wasn't interesting at all. But just as she was turning to go she heard something terrible indeed.

'You have an old boat,' said the fortune teller. 'In the next big wind she'll be blown away.'

Now FIonuala thought the word was 'goat', not 'boat'. With a scream of terror she ran away, for the wind was rising. Into the goat house she went and there she stayed. Days passed and she refused to come out.

'What's wrong with the old goat?' said the farmer. 'I've never seen her like this before.'

As time passed and nothing happened, Fionuala's fear grew less.

'It's probably Big Bill,' she thought, 'who'll be blown away,' and she looked forward to that with pleasure!

As night fell in Galway, Fionuala was still thinking about Jacko's forecast. 'Jacko,' she said, 'can you tell the future? Because if you can, you must know when we're going to find Daniel.'

'Me? Tell the future? What a daft question. Why do you ask?'

'The rain. You knew the *exact* time it would start.'

'I heard it on the radio. And you would have heard it too if you hadn't been dancing around.'

As they settled down for the night he spoke again. 'I wish,' he said, 'I *could* tell the future. Then I'd know when we're going home.'

In the morning a notice appeared on the Gallery wall:

PRIZEWINNERS ANNOUNCED TODAY

When the prizegiving began the Gallery was full. Fionuala stood at the back, trying to see what was happening on the platform. One by one the winners were announced. Her name was not called.

'Come on,' said Jacko, 'you didn't win,' and he began to leave.

At that moment a lady spoke. 'And now for the best picture of all,' she said, 'a portrait of a goat,' and she held Fionuala's picture high.

'I WON,' shrieked Fionuala, 'I knew I would.'

Down by the river she opened her prize. 'A trip for two,' it said, 'to the Clifden Connemara Pony Show. Coach leaves Eyre Square at 9 am tomorrow.'

'That'll be fun,' said Fionuala, 'I'd love to go.'

Jacko shook his head and sighed. '*Another* diversion. This expedition has gone all wrong. I should have stayed at home.'

10

The Connemara Pony Show

Next morning the coach drew up at Eyre Square and the prizewinners climbed in. Fionuala and Jacko were about to follow but the driver held up his hand.

'Where are *you* going?' he asked. 'No animals on this trip.'

'But I won a prize,' wailed Fionuala, 'for a picture of Daniel. He's my son.'

But the driver didn't understand a word she was saying. A boy and a girl heard the fuss and, being children, they knew what Fionuala had said. 'She's a prizewinner too,' they shouted. 'Her picture was brill!'

So Jacko and Fionuala were allowed to board the bus. It was a hot sunny day as they left Galway and drove over the river on the road to Oughterard. On and on they travelled, heading west, through the bogland where people were cutting turf. Bog-cotton drifted over dark, brown pools and the Twelve Bens appeared in the distance. They passed cottages and houses and sheep and ducks. On the roadside donkeys were grazing and Jacko craned his neck to see if he knew any of them.

'Where are the goats?' asked Fionuala, but there were no goats at all.

They came to Maam Cross and then passed Joyce's shop. In the fields, mares as grey as the Connemara rock grazed the grass which grew between the stones.

'Where are the trees?' Fionuala wondered, for there were no trees to be seen.

'Someone must have cut them all down,' said Jacko. Even he didn't know why there were no trees in Connemara.

Now the road was crowded with people and cars, all making for the show. The coach stopped outside Millers and the prizewinners got out. As Fionuala left, the driver gave her a strange look. She gave him a dazzling smile in return.

Music blared and people shouted as the crowd surged and shoved. 'Come to the House of Jericho,' a man called. 'Try your luck,' and he shuffled the cards.

Fionuala and Jacko hurried past the stalls and past the music. They followed the crowd and the crowd followed each other and it all led to the show. At the entrance gate people by the hundred were waiting to get in, but the animals slipped in with no trouble at all.

In the show-ring, all was activity and action. Ponies with shining coats and manes flowing free walked and trotted around in circles. People clapped the winners as they called to each other. Rivalry was in the air.

'You know,' said Fionuala as they stood watching the judging, 'Connemara Susie will be here.'

'Who's she?' asked Jacko, not much impressed.

'The brown mare's sister,' replied Fionuala. 'My friend at Sugarloaf Farm.'

And in one of the later classes Connemara Susie *was* there, and she won a prize.

'Hi, Susie,' called Fionuala, rushing up to her. But Susie gave Fionuala a very cold look and backed away.

'The brown mare sends love,' shouted Fionuala, 'to her sister Susie.'

'My name,' replied the mare, 'is CONNEMARA Susie. And who, might I ask, are you?'

'I'm Fionuala Cool-Boy,' said Fionuala grandly.

'I've heard of you,' said Susie. 'You're a menace,' and turning her back she trotted away.

'Stuck up,' said Fionuala, 'that's what horses are,' and Jacko agreed. 'I've had enough of them. I'm going to look at something else.'

'I'll stay here,' yawned Jacko, 'and doze.'

Fionuala wandered through the show, looking for something different but all there seemed to be were horses, horses, horses. Then a colourful display caught her eye. In an open-fronted shed, food and crafts were on view. Fionuala picked up a sweater and examined a scarf.

A voice said, 'That wool came from me,' and, smiling at her, was a nice, fat sheep.

'Did you mind,' asked Fionuala, 'when they took your coat away?'

'Not at all. I was terribly hot.'

In a hutch nearby was a fluffy angora rabbit. 'Look,' she called, 'see what I can do,' and she pointed to the softest wool of all.

'Did your fur make that?' asked Fionuala, much impressed.

'It did,' said the rabbit, 'and much, more more.'

A duck was sitting on a cosy straw nest. 'Would you like an egg?' she asked. 'I've loads to spare.'

'What nice animals,' thought Fionuala. 'And very very useful. Much more useful than horses.'

As she was looking at the food display, wondering whether she could take a piece of cake without being noticed, a cock crowed suddenly in her ear. 'Cock-a-doodle-doo,' he shouted.

'Is that the best you can do?' Fionuala asked. 'Frighten us to death?'

'Is it an argument you want?' replied the cock. 'To see who's best?'

So they argued about this and that and every time the cock won, he crowed. 'There's no doubt,' he said, 'goats are stupid.'

'I'll ask you a riddle,' said Fionuala, 'and we'll see who's stupid. Listen: why did the chicken sit on an axe?'

'I'm sure I know that,' said the cock. 'Just let me think.'

But though he thought very hard and his comb turned blood-red with effort, he couldn't guess the answer.

'To hatch-it, of course,' said Fionuala. 'Who's stupid, now?' And she departed as he leaped up and down with rage.

She rejoined Jacko just as the stallion class began. Into the ring they came, high-stepping and prancing, snorting and whinnying, sidling and rearing.

'My word,' said Fionuala. 'They're wild.' And she leaned over the rails to watch. As each stallion passed she made a loud remark – 'That one is far too fat, and that one's too thin.' The horses kicked and plunged as tension grew.

'Behave yourselves,' called Fionuala. 'Have you no manners?'

'Push off, you,' a passing stallion roared and he stuck his angry face over the rails.

Fionuala looked at his rolling eyes and his lashing feet. 'Useless old nag,' she shouted before she ran off, as the stallion broke loose. The crowd scattered but Fionuala had disappeared.

When Jacko found her she was standing in a leafy lane, admiring large motor-bikes.

'I'd love one of these,' she said. 'I'm sure I could ride it perfectly.' She felt the shiny paint and examined the wheels. Then she sat on each one in turn.

'Jacko,' she said with excitement in her voice, 'these bikes come from Sligo.' She pointed to a tiny flag on each which read SLIGO CLUB.

At that moment the bikers appeared. 'Just what we

need,' they said. 'A goat for a mascot and a donkey, too.' They crowded close, laughing.

In a trice Fionuala jumped on a bike but Jacko wouldn't budge. The bikers pushed and shoved but he stood firm.

'We'll take the goat,' said one, 'and leave the donkey.'

'You will not,' shouted Fionuala. 'He's my friend.'

'What's she saying?' they asked.

'I think,' said someone, 'that she won't leave the ass.'

After much scratching of heads and much chat the bikers hit on an idea. A side-car was fetched and fastened to the largest bike of all, and in Jacko went, as easy you please.

'Hold on,' called the boy who rode Fionuala's bike, and Fionuala wound her two front legs round his waist with a tight, tight grip.

With much revving and much noise the cavalcade of bikers left. They rode carefully through the crowded Clifden streets, past the show–grounds and the stalls, the hotels and the shops. Then, gaining speed, they left the town behind.

11
Westport House

The bikes roared along the road and the wind whistled by. Fionuala gasped and spluttered as her breath was whipped away, while Jacko shivered and shook as the side-car jolted along. The journey seemed to go on for ever, but eventually they stopped.

As Fionuala struggled off, her legs crumpled and she fell.

'The old goat's half dead,' said a biker.

'And the ass too,' said another as Jacko climbed from the side-car, badly shaken.

'Where will we put them for the night?' someone asked. 'We'll find a field,' said another and they did. Fionuala and Jacko were pushed into a small, stony field.

'Tomorrow we'll take you to the rally,' they shouted. 'You'll be a wow!' and, laughing heartily, they rode away.

Worn out by their journey, the animals slept, but at dawn Jacko woke.

'It's too early to get up,' protested Fionuala. 'I'm still half asleep.'

'Do you want another long ride to the rally?' asked Jacko. 'And who knows what they'll do there. Jumping over cars and looping the loop. I've had enough of that side-car, anyway.'

'You're right,' said Fionuala. 'Let's go.'

'We'll have to take a side road,' said Jacko. 'Otherwise they'll find us and make us go to the rally.'

As they limped along it was barely light. They were stiff and sore but Fionuala was in high spirits. 'To think,' she said, 'that we're practically in Sligo at last.'

'Sligo?' said Jacko. 'Look at that signpost. Can't you read?'

In dismay she looked at the signpost which had just come into view. It said: WESTPORT

'We haven't reached Sligo at all,' said Jacko in disgust. 'We're in another town altogether.'

Around a bend in the road large gates came into view. The notice beside them read: VISIT WESTPORT HOUSE.

'Look at that,' said Fionuala, brightening at once. 'Perhaps we'll find Daniel there,' and though Jacko protested she strode through the gates.

They went up a long winding driveway until they reached a very large house. A flight of steps led up to a heavy front door which stood open, inviting them in.

Westport House was very beautiful indeed. Fionuala and Jacko walked up the grand staircase, and admired the paintings on the walls. They saw the library and the shop where antiques were sold. They looked out through the windows at the river and the well-cut lawns. But there wasn't a sign or a sight anywhere of Daniel. At last, worn out, they went down to the basement to see the dungeon. It was spooky place but they were so tired that they fell fast asleep.

Fionuala awoke with a start. Staring at her was a large, woolly sheep

'How did you get in here?' he asked. 'The house is closed to the public today.'

'We came in through the front door,' replied Fionuala. 'Didn't you?'

'I did not,' answered the sheep. 'I came through the wall, the way I always do.'

'No one can come through walls,' said Fionuala scornfully. 'You're making it up.'

'Just watch then,' answered the sheep, and he disappeared through the wall behind him. Then he reappeared again.

'That's brilliant,' said Fionuala, much impressed. 'Could you teach me that trick?'

'It's no trick,' said the sheep. 'It's just something I can do.'

'Only ghosts can walk through walls,' said Fionuala,' and you don't look ghostly to me.'

'That's exactly what I am,' replied the sheep and he smiled a happy smile.

As Fionuala looked at him she felt quite faint.

'A g-g-go-ghost,' she stuttered. 'When did you b-be-come that?'

'Years ago,' replied the sheep. 'About a hundred I think.'

'Do you like being a ghost?' Fionuala asked, her courage returning.

'I love it,' replied the sheep. 'I can do anything I want. I can lie on the beds and sit in the chairs and watch TV and nobody knows I'm there. Before I became a ghost they used to chase me away if I even looked in at the windows of this house.'

'My friend Jacko nearly died,' said Fionuala, pointing to Jacko, who was still asleep. 'A golf ball hit him on the head. He's been acting strangely since then.'

'He'd make a dizzy ghost,' replied the sheep. 'Poor Jimmy was squashed by a tractor and he's been dizzy ever since.'

'Who's poor Jimmy?' asked Fionuala, looking around anxiously.

'He's a frog,' replied the sheep. 'He lives down by the lake.'

'You mean he's a ghost too?' asked Fionuala in amazement. 'Are there many of you here?'

'Loads of us,' replied the sheep. 'We have great fun together.'

At that moment Jacko awoke. 'Who are you talking to?' he asked, for he couldn't see the sheep at all.

'I'm talking to a sheep,' answered Fionuala. 'He's a ghost.'

Jacko looked at Fionuala in disbelief. 'You're batty,' he said. 'There's no one here.'

'Why can't Jacko see you?' Fionuala asked the sheep.

'Not everyone can,' he replied. 'You need to be tuned in to do that.'

'I'm very tuned in,' said Fionuala. 'I'm sure I could see every ghost there is,' and she felt quite excited by the thought.

'If you want to see more of us,' replied the sheep, 'I'll take you on a tour.'

'Stop talking to yourself, Fionuala,' said Jacko as they climbed the basement stairs.

Up in the Great Hallway they found the heavy front door locked. 'No problem,' said the sheep as he walked through the door and turned the key outside.

As the door creaked slowly open Jacko gasped. 'Who did that?' he asked, for his nerves were on edge.

'The sheep did,' replied Fionuala with admiration in her voice. 'He can do anything at all.'

As they walked through the grounds of Westport House they came to a sign which said: THIS WAY TO THE CHILDREN'S ZOO.

'I'm not going *near* any zoo,' said Jacko and he hurried on.

'Pity,' said the sheep, 'it's great fun down there playing tricks on the animals.'

On they walked and another sign said: AMUSE-MENTS THIS WAY.

'I'm not going there either,' said Jacko. 'Remember what happened at the amusements in Galway.'

At that moment a hooter sounded and round the corner, on the miniature railway, came a train crowded with happy children. Sitting in the last carriage, all waving, was a group of animals – a cow, a pig, four ducks and a hen.

'Here they come,' said the sheep in delight. 'The ghostly guys. I'm off to join them.'

'Can I come too?' called Fionuala.

'Not a chance,' answered the sheep. 'They wouldn't let you on – no animals – but they can't stop us guys at all. You see – they can't see us. He-he-he,' and he laughed loudly.

'It must be fun to be a ghost,' thought Fionuala but she didn't say it out loud, for Jacko was giving her very strange looks.

'How much further are we going?' he asked. 'It's clear that Daniel isn't here.'

As they started back towards the house the sheep appeared again, followed by his pals. As Fionuala laughed and joked with them Jacko looked at her in horror. 'Searching for Daniel has turned her head,' he thought and he was very distressed indeed.

At that moment a very-much-alive-dog came trotting along.

'Do you see that dog?' said the sheep. 'He likes to nip heels. Watch what I do to him,' and running up behind the dog he gave him a kick.

With a yelp the dog ran away and the ghostly guys roared with laughter.

'What happened to that dog?' asked Jacko in surprise

'The sheep kicked him,' replied Fionuala. 'It was great gas.'

'Must have been great gas for the dog,' said Jacko. 'How would *you* feel if someone kicked you ... No doubt about it,' he thought in dismay. 'She's turned very strange indeed. I'll have to get her away from here.' Aloud he said, 'Fionuala, we must leave for Sligo *now*.'

'But how are we to get there?' she asked.

'I know what you'll do,' said the sheep. 'Tomorrow morning early the gardener goes to Sligo with plants. I'll smuggle you into his van and you can travel go too.'

In the morning, before the sun was up, the gardener began to fill his van.

'It would be easier for you to travel if you were ghosts too,' said the sheep. 'We can travel the world in a second. Anywhere we please. Would you like me to arrange something deadly for you?'

'No thank you,' replied Fionuala hastily. 'We like it the way we are.'

The gardener finished packing his plants.

'Now,' said the sheep, 'I'll cause a disturbance and you can creep into the van.'

Nearby stood a pile of empty crates and the sheep tossed them high into the air. They fell to the ground with a crash.

'Janey Mac,' shouted the gardener. 'What's happening?' and he hurried to pick them up.

Fionuala and Jacko ran to the back of the van and without a second to spare they scrambled in. The gardener, hot and bothered, climbed into the driver's seat and the engine roared into life.

In front of the van stood the sheep, waving goodbye. The van leaped forward and Fionuala closed her eyes in horror as it hurtled right over him. She looked out through the back window and there he was, still waving. Jacko looked too, and for the first time he could see the sheep.

'Heavens above,' he thought, 'Fionuala was right! There *are* ghosts here. I'm glad we're leaving.'

It was a dull journey as the van had no windows so they couldn't see the mountains, the lakes and the bogs through which they were travelling. But at last they came to Sligo. On the outskirts the driver turned off the engine and sat for a moment to rest, and Fionuala and Jacko slipped quietly through the back door.

12
Sligo

As they walked along the road Jacko asked, 'How do we find Daniel? Where does he live? Do you know the way?'

'Let me think,' replied Fionuala. 'Just give me time,' but the minutes passed. and there was no answer to his questions.

'Fionuala,' said Jacko coming to a halt. 'Where in Sligo does your son live?'

'I really don't know,' she said at last, 'but I think it's in a castle.'

'You thought your relations in Glendalough lived in a castle, too,' said Jacko, 'but they didn't.'

'That was a mistake,' replied Fionuala, 'but my son might.'

On they walked not knowing which way to go. They came to a Tourist Office and Jacko stopped. 'We could ask here,' he said but the office was full.

'Join the queue,' hissed Jacko as Fionuala pushed to the front. When people saw a large white goat behind them they disappeared fast.

The man behind the counter had left his glasses at home. He peered at Fionuala, thinking he saw a white-haired lady. 'Sit down, Madam,' he said as he fetched her a chair. 'What can I do for you?'

'I'm looking for a castle,' replied Fionuala, 'my son lives there.'

The man gave Fionuala a puzzled look. 'I'm

sorry,' he said, 'could you say that again?'

'I'M LOOKING FOR A CASTLE,' replied Fionuala in a loud, loud voice.

'I'm going deaf,' thought the man, 'I don't understand a word she says.'

He took a deep breath and tried again. 'Where are you from?' he asked. 'What country?'

'I'm from Wicklow,' replied Fionuala. 'THAT'S IN IRELAND, YOU KNOW,' and her voice rose higher and higher still

'I understand,' said the man, who didn't understand at all. 'You're foreign.'

'I AM NOT,' shouted Fionuala. 'I'm as Irish as you,' and she gave him a very angry look.

At that moment Jacko appeared. The man looked at him and then at Fionuala and perspiration formed on his brow. 'I'm going mad,' he thought as he turned to a colleague for help. 'What do you do with foreigners?' he asked in despair. 'We only have a French dictionary and she sounds as if she came from Timbuctoo.'

'Give them a map,' replied his colleague without looking up.

Handing Fionuala a map the man croaked, 'Try the library – they might know,' and he hurried to serve someone else.

As they left, Fionuala was cross. 'Humans are thick,' she said. 'Very stupid indeed.'

The streets were busy with people going to work. The animals passed Lyons shop and the Silver Swan Hotel. They crossed the bridge and watched the water tumbling below. They walked along street after street but they never found the library. They came to

a cathedral and before Jacko could stop her Fionuala
hurried in.

'I went to church once,' she said. 'It was nice.'

Inside the cathedral people were deep in prayer.
Candles flickered and light shone through the
windows, casting colours on the floor. All was peace
and still. Jacko stood at the church door. Fionuala
tiptoed forward and, copying the people, she knelt
down to pray. But she didn't know any prayers so
she began to fidget and fuss. She looked at the
flickering candles and the flame beckoned her on.
She left her seat and moved to the front. In the
shadowy light, no one noticed her at all.

'I know what I'll do,' she thought. 'I'll make some
prayers up, that'll be fun.'

'God bless me,' she began, 'and God bless Jacko

and God bless my bike.' And she stopped to think. After a while she tried again.

'God bless the animals on Sugarloaf Farm,' she said, 'but not Big Bill or the cat. Perhaps God,' she continued, 'you could remove them for ever,' and she sat back well pleased.

But more prayers were forming in her mind. 'Thank you, God,' she said, for making me a goat and not a human. I'd hate to be that.'

Then she remembered Daniel and she was filled with guilt, for she hadn't prayed for him at all. 'God bless Daniel,' she whispered, 'and make us find him soon.'

At that moment a movement caught her eye. Something white was standing near. 'Could it be Daniel?' she gasped. 'Is my prayer answered so soon?'

But it wasn't Daniel at all only the priest preparing for Mass.

'I think,' she told herself, 'I'd better leave. All this peace and quiet is making me nervous.'

With head down she began to make her way out but something stood in front of her. An earwig was sitting on the floor, watching. Now Fionuala liked spiders and beetles and bugs, but of earwigs she was very afraid. She was afraid of their pincers and of how they scuttled from under stones. Most of all she feared they would run up her body and into her ear. She looked down, down at the earwig, and the earwig looked up, up at Fionuala who gave a scream.

'Keep away from me,' she shouted and over the seats she leaped and jumped until she reached the cathedral door.

Jacko was waiting outside. 'What happened?' he asked, when he saw her fear.

'Never you mind,' she answered as she walked on. But she had only taken a pace or two when to her amazement she came to another church – St John's Cathedral. Music was pouring out through the open door and she just had to go in.

'Come back,' called Jacko, but it was already too late. Inside, the organ swelled and boomed and voices soared. Fionuala stood at the back and listened. The choir was singing and the music was splendid. Fionuala liked music and she knew one hymn. As the choir practised she sang too: *'All things bright and beautiful, all creatures great and small.'*

The organ stopped. 'Someone,' said the organist, 'is singing the wrong tune.'

The choir looked at one another, shaking their heads.

'I heard it,' said the organist, *'distinctly.* We'll try again.' And they did. Fionuala hummed quietly and all was well.

'Now for our solo,' said the organist, and a girl called Avril began to sing.

'I could do that,' thought Fionuala, 'I'm sure I could.' She opened her mouth and her song poured out.

The organ stopped with a crash. 'Who's that?' Avril's husband Rowland called out. 'Who's trying to spoil our singing.'

He left the choir and walked down the aisle. Beside the font he stopped and stared.

'I can't believe this,' he called. 'It's an old white goat.'

'Get rid of her,' the choir shouted.

'We're all God's creatures,' Fionuala called indignantly, 'and I'm not old,' as Rowland threw her out.

Outside Jacko was waiting. 'What happened to you?' he asked when he saw her annoyance.

'Never you mind,' she answered, 'but I'm not going to church ever again,' and she walked angrily on as she muttered under her breath, 'Old indeed! I'm in my prime.'

A band playing a happy tune was coming down the Mall, shoulders straight and legs marching in time. The leader held a baton which he threw high in the air. The crowd gasped, afraid that it would fall, but he caught it every time.

'Come on, Jacko,' called Fionuala, 'this looks fun,' and she ran after the band. She skipped and twirled and sang. Jacko followed slowly, but as he watched Fionuala he could hardly bear to look, so sure was he that she would break a leg.

The band stopped at last before a gateway. Over it, a banner, flying in the breeze, said:

WELCOME TO SLIGO SHOW

The show-ground teemed with life. There were horses and dogs, pigs and sheep, but not one goat. 'Can you believe it?' said Fionuala in disgust.

'I can well believe it,' replied Jacko, 'and I know the reason why.'

They watched horses jumping and sheep being sheared. Fionuala laughed at the pigs and patted the dogs. She clapped and cheered and loved the fun. The show ended at last. Horses were loaded into trailers and sheep into vans. Dogs barked and pigs squealed, as the show ground emptied. Soon only the litter remained.

Over Knocknarea dark clouds formed as the rain began to fall. A leaflet blew against Fionuala's feet. She picked it up and began to read: 'Visit Woodville Farm, home of the Wood-Martin family for two hundred years. Follow the Nature Trail through the woods. Watch the animals grazing in the fields. We have cows and calves, pigs and lambs, chickens and ducks, donkeys and goats. . . ' Fionuala read no further.

'Jacko,' she said and her voice shook, 'I know *now* where Daniel lives,' and she left the show grounds at a run.

13

Woodville Farm

'Stop!' yelled Jacko as he tried to follow but Fionuala kept running and soon disappeared from sight

'That goat will kill me yet,' panted Jacko, and indeed his heart beat strangely and his head felt light. 'She can go where she likes,' he muttered. *'I'm* staying here,' and he turned his back to a tall hedge to shelter from the rain which now bucketing down.

Fionuala ran on and on. 'Hurry, Jacko,' she called, 'keep going,' but it was some time before she realised she was all alone.

'Where is he?' she wondered as she stared back along the empty road, 'I'd better wait.' But although she waited and waited, Jacko didn't come.

She trudged back along the road and it was almost dark before she found him.

'Are you ill?' she asked when she saw him huddled by the hedge.

'I'm half dead,' he replied. 'You're some friend.'

At last the rain eased and the moon appeared. Clouds scuttled by, casting eerie shadows

'We can't stay here,' said Fionuala, as a passing car splashed them.

'I can't go further,' replied Jacko. 'Here I'll have to stay.'

It was an uncomfortable night, for the rain started again. Cars passed with headlights blazing and they were splashed and dazzled all night long. Towards morning the animals woke with a start. Large black faces were peering through the hedge.

'Jacko,' she said, nudging him awake, 'we've got company.'

'Cows,' he yawned, 'and fat ones too.'

'That's an odd place to sleep,' said the cows. 'You must be strangers here.'

'We're going to Woodville Farm,' answered Fionuala, 'to visit my son.'

'You're on the wrong road,' said the cows and they told her the way.

They were both exhausted when they finally arrived at Woodville Farm.

'This isn't a castle,' said Jacko as they went through the gates.

'Maybe not,' answered Fionuala, 'but it's a very big house,' and her gaze wandered over the fields and the woods, for any minute she expected Daniel to appear. As they neared the house Jacko grew afraid.

'There might be dogs,' he said. 'Be careful.'

'Nonsense,' replied Fionuala. She went up to the front door and knocked loud and long. She hammered and banged but no one answered.

'What now?' asked Jacko.

'We wait,' replied Fionuala. But in a short time she grew bored. and decided to explore, looking at this and that and peering in through windows.

At last she came to a yard with a high wall and a strong gate. The sound of 'ba-a-ing' filled the air.

'Goats!' shouted Fionuala and with one kick she burst the gate in.

Inside the yard all was bustle and fuss, with sheep

everywhere and goats too. More goats peeped over
stable doors as they called loudly.

'Daniel!' Fionuala cried and she ran across the
yard. She looked into the stables one by one but
Daniel wasn't in any of them. The last stable of all
was in darkness but she could just make out the
shape of a white animal lying down.

'My son!' she bleated, 'I have found you at last!'
and, wrenching open the door, she clasped the figure
in a fond embrace.

Pandemonium broke out, for it wasn't Daniel at
all but an old white horse who was dozing in his stall.

In terror he kicked out, whinnying at the top of his
voice. Fionuala was flung to the floor and there she
lay.

'What's going on?' voices called. 'Has the horse
gone mad?' and two men appeared. When they saw
Fionuala they gasped in surprise.

'What goat is that?' they asked each other as they
carried her outside.

In the stable the horse shivered and shook. 'She
tried to kill me,' he wept, 'and I never saw her before.'

'Neither did we,' said the men, keeping their
distance for Fionuala was recovering fast.

'Jacko,' she called as she staggered to her feet, but
of Jacko there was no sign.

'Who are you?' asked the men. 'Why are you
here?'

'I'm Fionuala,' she replied, 'the Glendalough goat.
I've come to visit Daniel, my son,' and being farmers
the men understood exactly what she said.

'You mean Dan the Ran,' they said with a laugh.

'He's gone and good riddance we say.'

At those words Fionuala's world began to crumble. When the men saw her distress they spoke kindly. 'Come inside,' they said, 'and rest a while.'

So she went into the kitchen with Richard and Dick and they all sat round the table.

'Your son,' explained Dick, 'kept running away, so in the end we sold him.'

'Where to?' asked Fionuala, much upset.

'To Primrose Grange,' replied Richard, 'not far away.'

At that moment their wives arrived home. 'There's a large black donkey standing outside,' said Linda.

'That's Jacko,' replied Fionuala, 'he's my friend.'

'I'll bring him in,' said Elizabeth. 'He looks tired.'

'He doesn't like dogs,' said Fionuala, for there were dogs by the fire.

'These are nice fellows,' said Dick, and they were and Jacko didn't mind them at all.

And so the evening passed with great *craic*. Fionuala danced, while Jacko sang and Elizabeth played the fiddle.

'This is fun,' said Fionuala as she whirled around but at last even she grew tired.

'Stay for the night,' said Dick. 'Tomorrow, school children are visiting the farm.'

In the morning Fionuala and Jacko explored. Donkeys grazed in a large green field and with them was the old white horse. When he saw Fionuala he turned and trotted off.

'Keep away from that goat,' he shouted. 'She'll kill us all.'

A small grey donkey, braver than the rest, came close and stared in a nervous way.

'What a pretty sight!' said Jacko.

'She's fat,' said Fionuala, annoyed with the donkeys and the horse. 'And her legs are too short.'

The children had arrived and Richard took them into the wood. Fionuala was there already, munching and crunching as she tore off leaves. She licked the bark off the trees and trampled the wild flowers. The children laughed in delight but Richard wasn't at all pleased.

'Be off with you,' he shouted as he chased her away, 'get out of this wood.'

'How dare he talk to me like that?' thought Fionuala.

At the end of the wood was a pond full of ducks. When they saw Fionuala they quacked loud and long. 'There's that goat,' they said, 'who tried to kill the horse,' and they rushed out of the pond.

'Silly things,' said Fionuala as she watched them go.

On she went to see the cows and the calves. But when they saw her, they all disappeared fast. It was the same with the pigs and the sheep and the lambs. They all ran away in alarm.

'What's wrong with the animals on this farm?' Fionuala asked herself aloud.

A pheasant in the undergrowth heard what she said. 'I'll tell you what's wrong,' he said. 'There's a rumour around that you're a killer.'

'I've NEVER killed anything in my life,' shouted Fionuala, 'not even a fly.

'That's not what the rumour says,' answered the pheasant, and off he flew with a loud 'clock, clock'.

Fionuala went back to the house, feeling very annoyed. There something caught her eye. Beside the wall stood a wheelbarrow, all shiny and new. She looked at it long and hard. Then an idea came – and she liked that idea a lot.

Just then a little boy appeared. 'Would you like a ride?' she called.

'I would surely,' he answered and he climbed into the barrow. Off they went, with Fionuala pushing fast. They skidded round corners and whizzed along the straight paths.

Now other children appeared and they all wanted a ride. They laughed and screamed, urging Fionuala on and the barrow fairly flew. The last to go was a tiny girl in a pretty summer dress. As they turned a corner Fionuala slipped and the tiny girl fell out. But her landing was soft, for the dung heap was there and she landed right in the middle.

'Would you like me to dance?' Fionuala said when the wheelbarrow fun was over. So she leaped and jumped and kicked in the air and never had she danced so well. Elizabeth and Linda appeared, and when they saw the children, especially the tiny girl, they screamed and rushed them away to clean off the dung and dust.

'Get that goat!' shouted Richard. But she had already gone down the avenue to the gate where Jacko, luggage all packed, was waiting, anxious to be on the way.

'I've just thought of something,' said Fionuala. 'Wait – I'll only be a minute. I must tell that poor old horse that I'm sorry I scared him to death.'

Inside his stable, the white horse was dozing. When he heard Fionuala's voice he reared, with a scream of terror, and kicked the door off its hinges. Fionuala raced out on to the road for Primrose Grange

'Well, that's another place we'll never be asked to visit again,' said Jacko grimly.

14

Knocknarea

The road to Primrose Grange wound steeply, this way and that, climbing by the hill of Knocknarea. In a short while they could see the magnificent bay of Ballisodare spread out below them.

Primrose Grange, old and big, stood on the slopes of Knocknarea, its yellow walls and many windows shining in the morning sun.

'This house could tell some secrets,' said Jacko, as they pushed open the tall iron gate. Inside was a garden full of flowers, while over the roof-tops swallows swooped and dived.

'Rat-tat-tat.' Fionuala knocked on the stout front door.

'Ring-ring-ring,' went the bell as she pressed it hard. But the only sound was of birds singing.

'We'll try the yard,' she said, 'that's where they'll be.'

From a nearby shed came a sound of moo-ing and Fionuala looked cautiously in. Inside were cows all waiting to be milked. When they saw Fionuala they looked cross. 'What do you want?' they said. 'We don't like goats.'

'I don't like cows,' replied Fionuala. 'Big hulking brutes.'

'Take yourself off, then,' said the nearest cow, stamping in displeasure.

'Is Daniel here?' asked Fionuala more politely.

'He's my son.'

But the cows just laughed.

'What's so funny?' said Fionuala. 'Why do you laugh?'

'He left,' replied the cows, 'and aren't we glad.'

'Where did he go?' asked Fionuala in distress.

'Up there,' said the cows, pointing to Knocknarea.

'Not another climb!' groaned Jacko as they set off through the fields, jumping a wall and crossing a stile.

Up the mountainside they toiled, through heather and gorse until even Fionuala sat down, gasping for breath. From where they sat they could see a huge pile of stones on the top of the mountain

'Who put those stones there?' asked Fionuala. 'It's very strange.'

'That's Queen Maeve's tomb,' replied Jacko. 'The cows told me,' and as they rested he told her the story.

'Queen Maeve of Connacht was beautiful and proud. When her warriors went to battle she went too, with sword in hand, riding in her chariot. She and her husband Ailill had land and many possessions, but he owned the famous white-horned bull of Connacht and Maeve was jealous. In Ulster lived the brown bull of Cooley, who was as famous as the white bull, and Maeve determined to get him. The owner refused to part with him, so Maeve went to war with Ulster and her warriors stole him for her. When the bull of Connacht saw the brown bull of Cooley they fought each other all over the country, north, south, east and west. The whole land was in an uproar, till in the end the brown bull killed the

15

Coney Island

The path down the mountain was steep. Jacko slithered and slipped and grew afraid.

'Wait, Fionuala,' he called, 'I can't go so fast,' but she just bounded ahead.

Overhead a kestral hovered, with long tail and dark body. Her sharp eyes scanned the ground below, as rabbits and mice ran and even the song birds grew silent. When the kestrel saw Fionuala and Jacko she stopped hunting to watch. She swooped low and Jacko jumped with fright. 'You'll break a leg,' she said, 'if you follow that goat.'

'That's what I think,' panted Jacko. 'I'm too old for this.'

'That goat's in a hurry,' said the kestrel. 'Where's he going?'

'Mind your own business,' called Fionuala. 'It's nothing to do with you.'

That angered the hawk greatly and she dived at Fionuala with a loud cry. In terror she flung her body to the ground as the hawk flew off.

'Vicious bird,' said Fionuala as she scrambled to her feet. 'She could have killed me.'

'If you hadn't angered her,' replied Jacko, 'she might have told us where Daniel is, for hawks fly far and wide.'

'We don't need her help,' said Fionuala. 'We'll find him ourselves,' and off she went again but

white bull, but the effort was so great that he dropped dead.

'Who'd want to own a bull?' said Fionuala scornfully. 'Goats are better.'

On they climbed until they came to a tumbling stream where they stopped to drink and cool their tired feet. A little breeze fluttered and flowed, while a robin sang.

A hare hopped by. 'Hey, you,' called Fionuala. 'Do you know Daniel, my son?

'I know some goats all right,' said the hare. 'Dirty things they are too.'

'You've no manners,' said Fionuala, 'to speak like that.'

'Manners,' sniggered the hare, 'are what goats haven't got,' and off he hopped and disappeared from sight.

'I can't stand hares,' said Fionuala, 'they're useless creatures.'

'Fionuala,' said Jacko. 'Hares are very nice and they have a hard time. Why do you only like animals who think you are great?'

'Why not?' sniffed Fionuala, but she looked a bit ashamed.

As they climbed higher still a cold wind whipped over the mountaintop and the clouds threatened rain. They reached Maeve's tomb and it was very large indeed. And then at last they stood on the top of Knocknarea and all County Sligo could be seen – Benbulben, Lough Gill, the Ox Mountains and the sea.

They also saw something else. In a valley on the mountaintop, goats were grazing, their coats snowy white in the evening light.

'My son,' breathed Fionuala and she was off like a rocket. 'Daniel!' she shouted. 'My son! Your mother is here.'

'Be careful,' shouted Jacko, but it was already too late.

Like a whirlwind she descended upon the goats, scattering them fast. All except one, and she stood her ground.

'Get off our mountain,' she roared as she charged. Over and over Fionuala tumbled and the sky and the land whirled around her. When at last she stopped twirling and twisting, she lay there, quite dazed.

'We don't like strangers,' thundered the goat who had charged her. 'What do you want anyway?'

'I want my son Daniel,' whimpered Fionuala and

her tears began to fall.

'Is Daniel your son?' asked the goat in su and she helped Fionuala to her feet.

The other goats came slowly back. 'Daniel's they said.

Once more Fionuala's disappointment was felt. 'Where did he go?' she asked.

'Down there,' replied the goats pointing to hill and the sea.

As the sun set Fionuala and Jacko took the

'Be careful,' called the goats. 'Danger lur there.'

'Danger!' said Fionuala. 'What kind of that?'

'A huge bird with flashing eyes,' replied 'He flies night and day and never rests.'

'What does he do?' asked Jacko shaking

'He roars like a lion,' the goats answ many animals disappear.'

'Has Daniel disappeared?' Fionuala we what has happened to him?'

'No fear of that,' answered the goats. take care of himself.'

The sun set as Fionuala and Jacko goat herd disappeared from sight.

'Those are a wild lot,' Jacko said. ' too.'

'I agree with you there,' Fionuala rep ype of goat at all.'

slower now. By the time they reached the bottom of the mountain Jacko was tired,

'I must rest,' he said, 'or I'll die.'

Darkness crept over the mountain and the moon rose high. Jacko snored loudly but Fionuala couldn't sleep. Bats flew by and an owl called. She started and jumped, for her nerves were on edge. She thought of the bird with the flashing eyes and she longed for the day. But when dawn came at last, it was dismal with rain.

Jacko wakened and yawned and stretched. 'I've had a great sleep,' he said. 'Now for breakfast,' and he began to graze.

Fionuala was tired and wet and her spirits were low; she didn't feel like eating. As the rain eased they set off again and shortly passed some houses and gardens, bright with pretty flowers. Fionuala eyed them hungrily but Jacko hurried her past. Below them stretched Coney Island and Cummen strand. Fourteen stone pillars marked the way to the island, for when the tide came in the water was deep. On a small headland to the west stood Walker's Lodge, and further west still the ruins of Killaspugbron, an ancient Celtic church, showed stark against the sky.

'Let's go down there,' said Fionuala, and turning off the road she trotted along a steep, stony lane.

'Where are you going now?' called Jacko as they reached the shore.'

'To that house,' answered Fionuala, pointing to Walker's Lodge. 'Daniel might be there.'

Along the water's edge they walked, slithering and sliding, for the seaweed was wet, but there was no sign of Daniel at Walker's Lodge.

'Another fool idea,' said Jacko. 'I think we should go back to Strandhill and ask someone there.'

But Fionuala wasn't listening. She looked over the strand to Coney Island and excitement ran through her. 'Daniel is out there,' she said. 'I can feel it in my bones.' And she set off across Cummen strand.

'Come on, Jacko,' she called, 'this won't take long.' But it did. With each step their feet sank deep in the soft, wet sand, but at last they reached the island.

As they rested on the short island grass, rabbits scampered and played. 'Do you know my son Daniel?' called Fionuala, but they didn't answer.

'Deaf,' said Fionuala, 'that's what rabbits are. STUPID LONG EARS,' she shouted at the top of her voice.

'Mind you language,' said Jacko annoyed. 'Those words are insulting.'

'I wasn't insulting you,' said Fionuala. '*Your* ears are nice.'

They resumed their search again, with Fionuala calling, 'Daniel, your mother has come,' but although they searched the whole island there wasn't a sign of a goat.

Once more Fionuala was upset as they stood looking over the water to Rosses Point and the Metal Man, a huge statue of a sailor standing in the channel to the sea.

'What's that man doing?' Fionuala asked. 'Why is he there?'

'He's showing boats the deep water,' replied Jacko, 'See how he's pointing,' and he began to recite a poem:

Good morning Mr Metal Man,
I say, how do you do?
You're looking fine in whitelead pants,
And your coat of navy blue

'Who taught you that?' said Fionuala, much impressed.

'I heard it on TV,' replied Jacko

They went back across the island and everywhere rabbits played.

'If you're rude to them again,' warned Jacko, 'I'll go home to Wicklow.'

Fionuala longed to shout something, but as Jacko looked so stern, she didn't dare.

At the edge of the island, she stopped suddenly.

'Look,' she said and her voice shook. Jacko looked and gave a gasp of horror, for covering the strand where they had walked a short time before was water. Little waves tumbled and rolled as the tide came in.

'Quick,' said Jacko. 'If we follow the pillars we might make it to the mainland.'

'No,' wailed Fionuala, 'I couldn't, I'm afraid.'

'Then we'll stay on the island,' said Jacko, 'until the tide goes out.'

'No,' wailed Fionuala again. 'That bird with flashing eyes is somewhere here.'

'Well,' said Jacko, 'if you won't stay we'll have to go,' and off he strode.

Fionuala looked back at the island and all she could see were rabbits, dozens of them, all watching her. They were laughing and pointing and making rude faces.

'Pesty brutes,' she called, and making a rude face back she ran after Jacko.

The sand around the first pillar was dry. They passed it safely and then the second and the third. As they drew near the fourth little waves splashed over their feet. Fionuala gave a shriek.

'Do you want to go back?' asked Jacko. 'If you do, we must go now.'

Fionuala looked back at the island but the rabbits were still there, waving and jeering in a nasty way.

'We'll go on,' she gasped as more waves covered her feet.

As they went on, the water grew deeper still. It slapped against the pillars and crept up the animals' legs. As Fionuala looked towards the mainland she trembled with fear, for Cummen strand was a rolling, surging sea. But something else was happening, something frightening indeed; the light was fading. Soon it would be dark.

'We'll drown,' moaned Fionuala and Jacko, too, felt fear.

Overhead flew a curlew, its cry lonely and sad, Oyster-catchers skimmed the water, all making for the shore. Through the dusk the eighth pillar loomed close. The animals huddled beside it, unsure of what to do. As Fionuala looked at it hope grew.

'Look,' she said, 'the pillar has two ledges and a broad top.' With a leap and a jump she was up on the highest point. 'Come up, Jacko,' she called. 'Be quick.'

'I can't,' replied Jacko. 'I'm a donkey, not a goat.'

'I'll help you,' cried Fionuala leaping down again into the swirling water, for now she wasn't afraid.

She pushed and shoved, she pulled and tugged, but Jacko was old and stiff. He slithered and slipped and nearly fell but at last he made it to the first ledge and finally to the second.

Fionuala leaped once more to the top. 'We're saved,' she shouted and her voice carried over the water to Coney Island.

'It's that dratted goat,' said the rabbits. 'Hope she doesn't come back again,' and into their burrows they went for the night.

The hours of darkness slowly passed and Jacko grew cold and stiff. But Fionuala liked it on the pillar top. She sang, 'I'm the Queen of the Castle.... Amn't I great?' she shouted. 'I've saved you from a watery grave.'

'Whose fault is it that we're here anyway?' muttered Jacko to himself. 'I'd have stayed on the island.'

But Fionuala was in high spirits. 'I could get a medal for this,' she thought and she spent the night hours thinking happy thoughts.

At last the sky lightened and the tide went out. Jacko climbed stiffly from his ledge as Fionuala leaped down beside him.

'That was the worst night of my life,' he said, 'and I've had some bad ones in my time.'

At that moment, a loud noise was heard on the dawn air. A roaring, booming noise, as out of the grey sky a huge bird appeared. With outstretched wings it swooped lower and lower still.

'The bird with flashing eyes,' screamed Fionuala as she fell down in terror on the wet sand.

white bull, but the effort was so great that he dropped dead.

'Who'd want to own a bull?' said Fionuala scornfully. 'Goats are better.'

On they climbed until they came to a tumbling
stream where they stopped to drink and cool their
tired feet. A little breeze fluttered and flowed, while a
robin sang.

A hare hopped by. 'Hey, you,' called Fionuala.
'Do you know Daniel, my son?

'I know some goats all right,' said the hare. 'Dirty
things they are too.'

'You've no manners,' said Fionuala, 'to speak like
that.'

'Manners,' sniggered the hare, 'are what goats
haven't got,' and off he hopped and disappeared
from sight.

'I can't stand hares,' said Fionuala, 'they're useless
creatures.'

'Fionuala,' said Jacko. 'Hares are very nice and
they have a hard time. Why do you only like animals
who think you are great?'

'Why not?' sniffed Fionuala, but she looked a bit
ashamed.

As they climbed higher still a cold wind whipped
over the mountaintop and the clouds threatened
rain. They reached Maeve's tomb and it was very
large indeed. And then at last they stood on the top
of Knocknarea and all County Sligo could be seen –
Benbulben, Lough Gill, the Ox Mountains and the
sea.

They also saw something else. In a valley on the
mountaintop, goats were grazing, their coats snowy

white in the evening light.

'My son,' breathed Fionuala and she was off like a rocket. 'Daniel!' she shouted. 'My son! Your mother is here.'

'Be careful,' shouted Jacko, but it was already too late.

Like a whirlwind she descended upon the goats, scattering them fast. All except one, and she stood her ground.

'Get off our mountain,' she roared as she charged. Over and over Fionuala tumbled and the sky and the land whirled around her. When at last she stopped twirling and twisting, she lay there, quite dazed.

'We don't like strangers,' thundered the goat who had charged her. 'What do you want anyway?'

'I want my son Daniel,' whimpered Fionuala and

her tears began to fall.

'Is Daniel your son?' asked the goat in surprise and she helped Fionuala to her feet.

The other goats came slowly back. 'Daniel's gone,' they said.

Once more Fionuala's disappointment was heartfelt. 'Where did he go?' she asked.

'Down there,' replied the goats pointing to Strandhill and the sea.

As the sun set Fionuala and Jacko took their leave.

'Be careful,' called the goats. 'Danger lurks down there.'

'Danger!' said Fionuala. 'What kind of danger is that?'

'A huge bird with flashing eyes,' replied the goats. 'He flies night and day and never rests.'

'What does he do?' asked Jacko shaking with fear.

'He roars like a lion,' the goats answered, 'and many animals disappear.'

'Has Daniel disappeared?' Fionuala wept. 'Is that what has happened to him?'

'No fear of that,' answered the goats. 'Daniel can take care of himself.'

The sun set as Fionuala and Jacko left and the goat herd disappeared from sight.

'Those are a wild lot,' Jacko said. 'Unmannerly too.'

'I agree with you there,' Fionuala replied. 'Not my type of goat at all.'

15

Coney Island

The path down the mountain was steep. Jacko slithered and slipped and grew afraid.

'Wait, Fionuala,' he called, 'I can't go so fast,' but she just bounded ahead.

Overhead a kestral hovered, with long tail and dark body. Her sharp eyes scanned the ground below, as rabbits and mice ran and even the song birds grew silent. When the kestrel saw Fionuala and Jacko she stopped hunting to watch. She swooped low and Jacko jumped with fright. 'You'll break a leg,' she said, 'if you follow that goat.'

'That's what I think,' panted Jacko. 'I'm too old for this.'

'That goat's in a hurry,' said the kestrel. 'Where's she going?'

'Mind your own business,' called Fionuala. 'It's nothing to do with you.'

That angered the hawk greatly and she dived at Fionuala with a loud cry. In terror she flung her body to the ground as the hawk flew off.

'Vicious bird,' said Fionuala as she scrambled to her feet. 'She could have killed me.'

'If you hadn't angered her,' replied Jacko, 'she might have told us where Daniel is, for hawks fly far and wide.'

'We don't need her help,' said Fionuala. 'We'll find him ourselves,' and off she went again but slower now. By the time they reached the bottom of the mountain Jacko was tired,

'I must rest,' he said, 'or I'll die.'

Darkness crept over the mountain and the moon rose high. Jacko snored loudly but Fionuala couldn't sleep. Bats flew by and an owl called. She started and jumped, for her nerves were on edge. She thought of the bird with the flashing eyes and she longed for the day. But when dawn came at last, it was dismal with rain.

Jacko wakened and yawned and stretched. 'I've had a great sleep,' he said. 'Now for breakfast,' and he began to graze.

Fionuala was tired and wet and her spirits were low; she didn't feel like eating. As the rain eased they set off again and shortly passed some houses and gardens, bright with pretty flowers. Fionuala eyed them hungrily but Jacko hurried her past. Below them stretched Coney Island and Cummen strand. Fourteen stone pillars marked the way to the island, for when the tide came in the water was deep. On a small headland to the west stood Walker's Lodge, and further west still the ruins of Killaspugbron, an ancient Celtic church, showed stark against the sky.

'Let's go down there,' said Fionuala, and turning off the road she trotted along a steep, stony lane.

'Where are you going now?' called Jacko as they reached the shore.'

'To that house,' answered Fionuala, pointing to Walker's Lodge. 'Daniel might be there.'

Along the water's edge they walked, slithering and sliding, for the seaweed was wet, but there was no sign of Daniel at Walker's Lodge.

'Another fool idea,' said Jacko. 'I think we should go back to Strandhill and ask someone there.'

But Fionuala wasn't listening. She looked over the strand to Coney Island and excitement ran through her. 'Daniel is out there,' she said. 'I can feel it in my bones.' And she set off across Cummen strand.

'Come on, Jacko,' she called, 'this won't take long.' But it did. With each step their feet sank deep in the soft, wet sand, but at last they reached the island.

As they rested on the short island grass, rabbits scampered and played. 'Do you know my son Daniel?' called Fionuala, but they didn't answer.

'Deaf,' said Fionuala, 'that's what rabbits are. STUPID LONG EARS,' she shouted at the top of her voice.

'Mind you language,' said Jacko annoyed. 'Those words are insulting.'

'I wasn't insulting you,' said Fionuala. '*Your* ears are nice.'

They resumed their search again, with Fionuala calling, 'Daniel, your mother has come,' but although they searched the whole island there wasn't a sign of a goat.

Once more Fionuala was upset as they stood looking over the water to Rosses Point and the Metal Man, a huge statue of a sailor standing in the channel to the sea.

'What's that man doing?' Fionuala asked. 'Why is he there?'

'He's showing boats the deep water,' replied Jacko, 'See how he's pointing,' and he began to recite a poem:

Good morning Mr Metal Man,
I say, how do you do?
You're looking fine in whitelead pants,
And your coat of navy blue

'Who taught you that?' said Fionuala, much impressed.

'I heard it on TV,' replied Jacko

They went back across the island and everywhere rabbits played.

'If you're rude to them again,' warned Jacko, 'I'll go home to Wicklow.'

Fionuala longed to shout something, but as Jacko looked so stern, she didn't dare.

At the edge of the island, she stopped suddenly.

'Look,' she said and her voice shook. Jacko looked and gave a gasp of horror, for covering the strand where they had walked a short time before was water. Little waves tumbled and rolled as the tide came in.

'Quick,' said Jacko. 'If we follow the pillars we might make it to the mainland.'

'No,' wailed Fionuala, 'I couldn't, I'm afraid.'

'Then we'll stay on the island,' said Jacko, 'until the tide goes out.'

'No,' wailed Fionuala again. 'That bird with flashing eyes is somewhere here.'

'Well,' said Jacko, 'if you won't stay we'll have to go,' and off he strode.

Fionuala looked back at the island and all she could see were rabbits, dozens of them, all watching her. They were laughing and pointing and making rude faces.

'Pesty brutes,' she called, and making a rude face back she ran after Jacko.

The sand around the first pillar was dry. They passed it safely and then the second and the third. As they drew near the fourth little waves splashed over their feet. Fionuala gave a shriek.

'Do you want to go back?' asked Jacko. 'If you do, we must go now.'

Fionuala looked back at the island but the rabbits were still there, waving and jeering in a nasty way.

'We'll go on,' she gasped as more waves covered her feet.

As they went on, the water grew deeper still. It slapped against the pillars and crept up the animals' legs. As Fionuala looked towards the mainland she trembled with fear, for Cummen strand was a rolling, surging sea. But something else was happening, something frightening indeed; the light was fading. Soon it would be dark.

'We'll drown,' moaned Fionuala and Jacko, too, felt fear.

Overhead flew a curlew, its cry lonely and sad, Oyster-catchers skimmed the water, all making for the shore. Through the dusk the eighth pillar loomed close. The animals huddled beside it, unsure of what to do. As Fionuala looked at it hope grew.

'Look,' she said, 'the pillar has two ledges and a broad top.' With a leap and a jump she was up on the highest point. 'Come up, Jacko,' she called. 'Be quick.'

'I can't,' replied Jacko. 'I'm a donkey, not a goat.'

'I'll help you,' cried Fionuala leaping down again into the swirling water, for now she wasn't afraid.

She pushed and shoved, she pulled and tugged, but Jacko was old and stiff. He slithered and slipped and nearly fell but at last he made it to the first ledge and finally to the second.

Fionuala leaped once more to the top. 'We're saved,' she shouted and her voice carried over the water to Coney Island.

'It's that dratted goat,' said the rabbits. 'Hope she doesn't come back again,' and into their burrows they went for the night.

The hours of darkness slowly passed and Jacko grew cold and stiff. But Fionuala liked it on the pillar top. She sang, 'I'm the Queen of the Castle.... Amn't I great?' she shouted. 'I've saved you from a watery grave.'

'Whose fault is it that we're here anyway?' muttered Jacko to himself. 'I'd have stayed on the island.'

But Fionuala was in high spirits. 'I could get a medal for this,' she thought and she spent the night hours thinking happy thoughts.

At last the sky lightened and the tide went out. Jacko climbed stiffly from his ledge as Fionuala leaped down beside him.

'That was the worst night of my life,' he said, 'and I've had some bad ones in my time.'

At that moment, a loud noise was heard on the dawn air. A roaring, booming noise, as out of the grey sky a huge bird appeared. With outstretched wings it swooped lower and lower still.

'The bird with flashing eyes,' screamed Fionuala as she fell down in terror on the wet sand.

16
Lough Gill

When Fionuala opened her eyes again Jacko was bending over her. 'Are you all right,' he said. 'Can you stand up?'

'That bird,' whispered Fionuala as she staggered to her feet, 'it nearly had me.'

'That wasn't a bird,' replied Jacko. 'That was a plane coming in to land.'

'What nonsense,' said Fionuala recovering fast. 'There's no airport here.'

'Yes there is,' answered Jacko, 'it's over there.'

'I don't believe you,' said Fionuala. 'I'm leaving this place and never coming back.'

Along the shore she ran, over the sandhills and straight on to the runway. There stood the plane, its lights still flashing and its engine running, and Fionuala felt very foolish indeed.

'How was I to know,' she muttered, 'there was an airport here?' but being a curious goat she had to take a closer look.

Sean was sitting in the Control Tower when Fionuala appeared on the runway.

'Holy smoke,' he shouted, 'there's a goat down there.'

As Fionuala reached the plane a small van tore over the tarmac and screeched to a halt. 'Clear the runway,' bellowed the driver, 'a plane is going to land.' He shoved Fionuala into the van and they drove off fast.

Sean's voice came over the radio. 'There's a donkey on the runway too.' Sure enough, Jacko had appeared.

Once more the van braked and Jacko was pushed in. Back over the runway they raced with only seconds to spare, for the plane was approaching fast. With a roar that shattered the air and with all its lights flashing, the plane came in, over the pillars and Cummen strand, lower and lower, until its wheels touched down.

'I'd like to fly a plane,' said Fionuala. 'I'm sure I'd do it well,' and she opened the van door.

'Stay where you are,' roared the driver and, slamming the door shut, he drove off.

'Where is he taking us?' wondered Jacko. 'We've done no harm.'

They sped along the road, through Sligo and on to Lough Gill. At Half Moon bay the driver pushed the animals out. 'You'll cause no trouble here,' he said. 'Why don't you take a boat? Goat Island is just out there.' Laughing at his joke, he left.

In the morning sunshine Goat Island showed clear.

'Goat Island!' cried Fionuala. 'Of course! That's where he'll be. Why didn't I think of it before? Now, to find a boat. That shouldn't be hard,' and it wasn't for a boat was moored near. Oars and all.

With skilful, even strokes they glided along and Goat Island drew near. Faster and faster Fionuala rowed, until the boat scraped on the shore. She leaped out, leaving Jacko behind, and tore all over the island.

'Daniel,' she shouted, 'are you here?' But there were no goats on Goat Island at all.

With a heavy heart she returned to the shore. Jacko was looking at the lake, for far out, bobbing up and down on the water, was their boat.

'Why didn't you tie it up?' asked Fionuala crossly.

'How could I?' answered Jacko. 'You left the rope behind.'

'We've been shipwrecked,' said Fionuala, and she felt rather pleased.

'We have not,' replied Jacko. 'We've just lost our boat.'

'Same thing,' said Fionuala. 'What a story this will make!'

'If we're ever found,' replied Jacko. 'Perhaps we never will.'

'There's plenty to eat,' said Fionuala looking at the long grass and nettles, for no animal had grazed there for years.

'I'll keep watch,' said Jacko, ' in case a boat comes by.' But not one boat appeared.

When evening approached the rain began to fall. It drifted over the lake blotting out the far shore. As darkness came, bird calls floated eerily through the mist.

'It's lonely here,' said Fionuala, 'I hope there aren't ghosts.'

'Drip, drip,' went the leaves as the animals shivered and shook, for a cold wind blew. Something rustled in the undergrowth and ran over Fionuala's feet.

'Help!' she shrieked, as a large rat scuttled away.

The night passed, dreary and cold, and still the

rain came down. 'We'll have to swim,' said Jacko.

'I can't,' said Fionuala, 'I'd rather die,' and she looked with horror at the dark, heaving waves.

The rain had eased when a sound came over the lake. It throbbed and vibrated. A boat was approaching fast.

'Rescue!' cried Fionuala. 'I knew someone would come.' But the boat passed by.

'I don't believe this,' said Fionuala. 'What a rotten trick.'

But all was not lost, for a second boat appeared. Its engines stopped, a rope was thrown ashore, and out jumped chattering people. They streamed past the animals without even a glance.

'Who are these people?' Fionuala wondered. 'Why are they here?'

The crowd had grown quiet, all except one man. With raindrops clinging to his beard, he began to speak, pointing and gesturing towards the far shore.

'He's telling a story,' said Jacko. 'Isn't that odd?'

'He's reciting poetry,' answered Fionuala, 'I think it's a kind of school.'

'Who'd have a school out here?' said Jacko. 'That's daft.'

Suddenly, as quickly as they had come, everyone left. They rushed back to the boat, followed by Fionuala and Jacko.

'To Church Island,' someone shouted and they went across the lake. At Church Island the same performance took place. A tour of the island and then a poetry reading.

'Poetry is nice,' said Jacko. 'Why don't you listen?'

So Fionuala listened and she didn't like it at all.

The man with the beard was intoning:

A hive for the honey bees. . .

'He's talking about bees,' she said in alarm. 'If there are bees here, I'm off.'

As she waited in the boat she remembered poems she knew. 'I'll say some for those people,' she thought, 'that'll give them a nice surprise.'

As they left Church Island she stood up and the boat rocked and swayed as she began to recite:

Once there was a goat,
A very pretty goat. . .

but she got no further.

'SIT DOWN,' roared everyone, 'you'll turn us over.'

'What cheek,' she said to Jacko and she felt most annoyed.

On they went and the Isle of Innisfree drew near. Not a word was spoken as they all stepped ashore. Then a sob was heard and then another.

'What's wrong with them?' asked Jacko. 'Why are they sad?'

'It must be the poetry,' said Fionuala. 'I'll cheer them up.' And she sang:

> *It's a long way to Tipperary,*
> *It's a long way to go.*

'GET RID OF THAT GOAT,' someone shouted. 'She's ruining our day.'

'Where did she come from?' asked another. 'She and the donkey just appeared.'

Then a young man spoke and he was very angry indeed. 'I haven't come here,' he said 'to have the poet Yeats insulted.' And everyone agreed.

'Calm down,' said the bearded man. 'We'll get rid of these animals and do the whole tour again.'

'I should think so,' voices murmured.

The boat turned for the mainland and as they reached the shore, another boat appeared. But something was wrong with that one. It was low in the water and its engines had stopped. Slowly but surely, it was sinking. Down it went with a 'gurgle' and a 'glug' in two feet of water and a few damp wet people struggled ashore.

Fionuala looked at them closely. 'That's the boat that passed by Goat Island,' she said, 'and wouldn't rescue us. Serves them right!'

The animals clambered ashore and as the tour

boat turned back for Innisfree, Fionuala began to sing.

> *Once there were some people,*
> *Some very silly people*

'Stop it,' said Jacko wearily, and without a backward glance he left Lough Gill.

17

Parke's Castle

Fionuala was depressed as they trudged along the road from Lough Gill.

'I think we'll go home,' she said. 'Daniel is not to be found.'

Jacko was amazed; this wasn't like Fionuala at all.

'Look,' he said, trying to cheer her up, 'there's a castle. Let's go and explore.'

'No,' replied Fionuala, 'what's the point.'

'I thought you liked castles,' said Jacko. 'You talk about them enough.'

'I don't like them now,' answered Fionuala, 'not any more.'

Outside the castle a queue had formed, all waiting to get in. A large notice read:

PARKE'S CASTLE
ONCE OWNED BY THE O'RORKES.

As they joined the queue Fionuala was silent, with head down. She didn't speak.

'Listen,' said Jacko, 'I hear music,' and sure enough a guitar was being played.

As they approached the guitarist, the music faltered and stopped. Fionuala raised her eyes and looked into his. Eyes the colour of hers looked back, and the whole world spun round.

'Mother!' croaked the guitarist, and he caught her as she fell.

'My son,' she whispered as she fainted away.

When Fionuala recovered, she was in a very nice room. A fire burned in the hearth for the air was chill. Daniel stood at a window looking out. When he heard her move he hurried to her side.

'Mother,' he said, 'are you all right?'

'I feel great,' answered Fionuala, jumping up.

The fire flickered, casting shadows on the walls, for the room was growing dark. Outside the wind moaned but Fionuala only felt joy that Daniel was found.

And so they talked far into the night. She felt pride as she looked at her son. 'Just like his father,' she thought. 'So handsome and strong.'

At last it was time for bed. 'You'll stay for a week,'

said Daniel, 'or maybe two?'

'We'll stay for the summer,' answered Fionuala. 'For two months or more.'

'Remember, I've a job to do,' said Daniel. 'I'm busy all the time.'

'I'll help you,' replied Fionuala, 'I could do that well,' and she went happily to bed.

Daniel was up early and Fionuala was too. In his well-cut trousers and stylish shirt, he was preparing for the day. Fionuala followed him round the castle and was impressed by all she saw. She walked through the arched entrance and admired the stairs. She examined the kitchen and looked at the stores. She exclaimed with wonder at the Great Hall and tried the window-seats. She climbed to the bed-chambers and admired the view, and she thought how grand it was for Daniel to live there.

'How impressed the goats on Sugerloaf Farm will be,' she thought. 'What a lot I'll tell them when I get home.'

Then another thought came and it was an exciting one indeed. 'Perhaps I'll stay here with Daniel and never go home,' and she shivered with delight

Every day tourists queued outside the castle, while Daniel played his guitar. Fionuala clapped and cheered, thinking, 'What a great musician, I hope he gets a tip.' And he always did.

She organised the queue and hustled them in, and sometimes she sang and danced.

'Listen, Ma,' said Daniel, 'leave the tourists to me.'

'But I like to help,' replied Fionuala. 'It's fun.'

Each evening, when the day's work was done, they

sat by the fire and talked.

'What did you do today, Jacko?' Fionuala would ask day after day.

'I slept,' said Jacko, 'this weather makes me tired.'

After a few days Fionuala grew quiet.

'What's wrong, Ma?' asked Daniel. 'Are you ill?'

'Certainly not,' said Fionuala, 'I've a lot on my mind,' for a plan had formed in her head.

'When your Ma goes quiet,' said Jacko, 'there's trouble brewing.'

The following night Fionuala didn't sleep. Her plan was ready, and it was time to put it to the test. It was still dark when she awoke, for there was much to do. Round the castle she went, checking this and that.

As the day's tour began she ran ahead. When the tourists reached the kitchen they found a notice on the door: 'Fresh water from the lake, 50p a cup.' The day was hot and the tourists thirsty, so they bought every drop.

Up in the Great Hall the door was tightly shut. 'See the castle ghost,' said a sign outside, '50p each.'

'How exciting,' said the tourists and they all paid up.

It was dark inside the Great Hall. A hush fell as the crowd waited. In one corner a light appeared and a ghostly moan was heard. Across the hall it drifted, growing louder and louder still, ending in a blood-curdling yell.

'How terrifying!' said everyone, but more was to come. A white figure appeared which shimmered and shone, its eyes glowing like fire.

'I must say,' said an awed voice, 'the audio-visual aids are great.' And everyone agreed.

When the tourists entered the bedchamber it was dark indeed, for thick brown paper covered the windows.

'50p to see the view,' said a notice and the tourists peeped out.

'Ma,' hissed Daniel, 'THIS WON'T DO.'

'It'll do very well,' replied Fionuala, 'and I'm not finished yet.'

At the entrance hall on the way out, Fionuala barred the way. 'A souvenir of your visit,' said neat little cards. 'Buy a stone from Lough Gill.'

'What a splendid idea!' said everyone, as they paid 50p each.

That evening a man from the Tourist Board arrived.

'There's been a complaint,' he said, 'about that old goat.'

The next day when the tourists arrived Jacko led a protesting Fionuala away.

'Don't bring her back,' pleaded Daniel, 'until the tourists have gone. Show her the sights of Sligo.'

The weeks passed and Fionuala and Jacko saw everything there was to be seen. They rowed on Lough Gill and sailed at Rosses Point. They climbed the mountains and walked on the sands. They camped on Cottage Island and picnicked at Strandhill.

They also made a special tour of all the homes of the poet Yeats, and Jacko tried his hand at being a guide. At Parke's Castle he had listened with admiration to the tour guide. 'I could do that,' he thought. Now he had his chance.

'This is Merville where Yeats's grandparents, the Pollexfens lived,' he told Fionuala.

'Pollexfen? What an odd name,' she repled, admiring the splendid grey stone building.

'Old Pollexfen was a sea captain and had treasures from all over the world,' continued Jacko. 'Chinese paintings on rice-paper, ivory walking-sticks from India, coral from Australia. He even had a jar of Jordan water. All his children were baptised with that.'

'Jordan water,' said Fionuala. 'What's so special about that? Wouldn't Wicklow water do?'

'Fionuala,' said Jacko severely. 'Don't keep asking stupid questions. The tourists at Parke's Castle would never ask such silly things.'

'Sorry,' she said meekly, for she was most impressed by Jacko's knowledge.

They moved on to Charlemont House, a huge house on top of a hill.

'What a chilly place to live,' said Fionuala shivering. 'The goat house at Sugarloaf farm would be warmer.'

'No one is talking about goats,' scolded Jacko. 'We're discussing Yeats.'

So on they went to Rathedmond on the other side of Sligo and then to Elsinore at Rosses Point.

'Smugglers hung out here,' said Jacko. 'It's haunted. A dead smuggler comes back now and then and gives three raps as a signal.'

They were standing in the ruined interior, looking out at the bleak landscape dotted with leafless hawthorn bushes, as the winds of autumn howled

around the chimneys. Then all at once they heard it:
KNOCK, KNOCK, KNOCK.

'The smuggler's ghost,' screamed Fionuala,
rushing from the place. And indeed Jacko wasn't far
behind her. And they didn't slow down until they
had left Rosses Point far behind.

On their way home they passed a small newsagent.
A placard outside the shop caught Fionuala's eye:

NO SIGN YET OF THE MISSING PAINTINGS

'Jacko,' she shouted, 'Do you know what I think?'

'No,' said Jacko, 'but hurry up or we'll be late for
our oats'

'Wait a minute!' Fionuala nipped into the shop
and began to read the report under the headline:

No news yet about the valuable paintings stolen from one of Ireland's Great Houses ... thieves cut them from frames for easier getaway ... believed to be hidden somewhere on the west coast ... 'Lady at a Spinet' the most valuable painting ... garda in charge of enquiry feels sure someone will come forward to claim big reward...

And there beside the article was a photograph of the painting Fionuala carried on her back in the plastic bag. She grabbed the newspaper just as the owner appeared to chase her away.

'Jacko!' she screamed as she ran to catch up with him. 'I knew it. The painting of the lady and the strange-looking piano. There's a huge reward. And I know where the rest are.'

Jacko was convinced when Fionuala unrolled the painting back at the castle and they compared it with the one in the newspaper.

'Isn't it lovely?' she said.

'And valuable too,' answered Jacko.

Daniel, who had just come in, looked briefly at the painting. 'When you live in a castle,' he said, 'you get used to paintings. When you seen one, you've seen them all.'

'We'll have to get in touch with Patrick,' Fionuala said happily. 'How do we get our reward?'

'Go to the Garda Station,' said Daniel, 'they'll take all the particulars.'

'Yes,' Fionuala answered, 'and they probably won't understand what we are trying to tell them. Humans are thick!'

But when they went to the Garda Station, to their

amazement, the guards understood everything they said.

The painting was handed over and Fionuala drew a sketch of the cave in which the other paintings were hidden. Now she and Jacko were the centre of attention. She even got a beautiful bouquet of dahlias and lilies, which she sniffed in delight.

'Don't eat it!' hissed Jacko as she buried her face in the blooms.

'Smile,' called yet another photographer.

So they went on smiling and their pictures appeared in all the papers and they were shown on TV. The reward was to be sent on to their homes.

'I'm famous at last,' said Fionuala, 'I always knew I would be.'

The summer was over and the days were growing short. Fionuala noticed that Daniel was getting restless.

'Ma,' he said one evening, 'my job will soon end here. Then I'll be off to the hills.'

'You're coming home,' said Fionuala in delight. 'To the Wicklow hills.'

'No,' replied Daniel. 'My home's in Sligo now. I'm going to the Ballygawley mountains. You can come if you like. And Jacko too.'

Before Fionuala could answer Jacko broke in. 'Go up into the mountains? Certainly not! I'm going home. To Enniskerry House.'

He took a letter out of his pocket. It was from his owners. They had seen Jacko and Fionuala on TV.

'Dear Jacko:' he read, 'Come home before the winter days begin. Be at Sligo Airport next Thursday.'

'You're going home by PLANE!' said Fionuala and her eyes danced with delight. 'Then I'll go, too.'

And so it was all arranged.

18
Home

The departure day arrived. The castle was empty, the tourists gone. The windows were closed and the doors securely locked.

'This castle is cold,' said Fionuala, 'I'm sure it's damp.'

At the entrance Daniel waited, his guitar slung over his back.

Fionuala looked at him in shocked disbelief. Gone were his well-cut trousers and his stylish shirt. His jeans were ragged, his sweater old and Doc Martins covered his feet.

'Your nice clothes,' she gasped, 'where have they gone?'

'They went with the job,' replied Patrick. 'Good riddance I say.'

And so the animals left Parke's Castle. Once more they walked the Sligo roads. They passed Woodville Farm and Primrose Grange. The saw Knocknarea and Queen Maeve's tomb and at last, footsore and weary, they came to Strandhill.

At the airport a plane was waiting, a neat little plane with just four seats. Fionuala looked at Daniel with sadness in her eyes. 'There's room for you, son,' she said.

'I can't come, Ma,' he answered, 'I'm off to the mountains to find a wife.'

'A wife,' said Fionuala and she brightened at once.

'I'll come back for the wedding.'

The plane door closed, the seat-belts clicked shut.

'This is living,' thought Fionuala as they got ready to fly.

Down the runway the little plane went, faster and faster still, as Jacko covered his eyes. Then it gently took to the air and rose high in the sky. On the runway Daniel watched them go. With a sigh of relief he made for the hills.

As the plane set course Fionuala was sad.

'Look out of the window,' said Jacko, 'that will cheer you up.' And it did. Fionuala loved it all, the fields and rivers, the towns and farms.

'I wish,' she said, 'I could try to fly the plane.'

'Don't touch it,' screamed Jacko, 'you'll make us crash.' And he longed for the journey to end.

But the journey did end at last as Enniskerry House came in sight. Below flew the windsock, as lower and lower the pilot took his plane until, with a gentle bump, they landed.

'Home at last,' said Jacko 'I never thought I'd live to see the day.'

'The holiday did you good,' said Fionuala.

'Holiday? That was no holiday. That was hard work.'

'Well, whatever it was, you're looking much better. Leaner, fitter. You should take more exercise.'

And when Jacko passed by a mirror, he was amazed to find that she was absolutely right. He looked years younger.

He also thought of something else; he hadn't had a nightmare about the horses for ages. 'Maybe there's something in this exercise business,' he told himself.

And so Fionuala went home to Sugarloaf Farm. The goats crowded round to hear her story and even Big Bill stayed still.

As dusk fell she walked the farm to see if anything had changed. The brown mare was in her stable, the cat asleep in the hay. The ducks were on the pond and the bees in the meadow.

But something was new. A small shed had been built and, as Fionuala peered in, her heart beat fast, for standing there was a shiny new motor-bike.

Darkness fell and the goats settled down for the night. Gentle breathing could be heard and a snore or two, but Fionuala was still awake. Already her holiday was slipping from her mind, for something else was filling her thoughts and that something was the motor-bike. Then another thought came and it was an exciting one indeed.

'I'll visit Jacko every day, for on the motor-bike the journey won't take a minute. We'll travel round the county and see all the towns.'

With these happy thoughts she fell asleep. It was going to be a busy year!